MONTGOMERY - BILLY WHISKERS

"LOOK HERE, THAT IS MY GOAT!"

See p. 92

BILLY WHISKERS

THE AUTOBIOGRAPHY OF A GOAT

by
Frances Trego Montgomery

Illustrated by W. H. Fry

DOVER PUBLICATIONS, INC., NEW YORK

This Dover edition, first published in 1969, is an
unabridged and unaltered republication of the work
originally published by the Saalfield Publishing Company, Akron, Ohio, in 1902. Illustrations facing pages
40, 41, and 150 were originally in color but are here
reproduced in black and white.

Standard Book Number: 486-22345-0
Library of Congress Catalog Card Number: 70-81803

Manufactured in the United States of America
Dover Publications, Inc.
180 Varick Street
New York, N.Y. 10014

CONTENTS

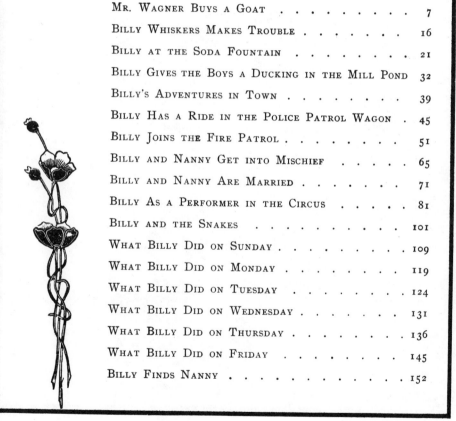

ILLUSTRATIONS

Mr. Wagner Buys a Goat

 R. Wagner lived about two miles from a small town, and he thought it would be nice for his boys to have a little goat cart, so they could drive into town for mail and do errands for the family.

Without saying anything to his family, he appeared one evening leading a nice, docile looking, long-bearded Billy goat, hitched to a beautiful new red wagon.

Of course, the boys were wild with delight, and their mother disgusted, for she predicted that he would be more bother than he was worth, and would eat up all the things in the garden. They answered her that they would take good care that he never got loose, and that no wrong would happen, if she would only let them keep the goat. So with many misgivings she gave her consent, and Billy was led to the stable behaving like a lamb.

The boys christened him Billy Whiskers immediately, on account of his long white beard. It being a warm night, they tied him near a shed, so if it rained he could go under it for protection, and giving him some grass and a bucket of water, they went to bed to dream of the fun they were going to have the next day with Billy Whiskers.

It was five hours later when Billy awakened from his first long sleep, and feeling refreshed, thought he would take a look around. It was bright moonlight, and as all the lights were out in the house, he knew he would not be disturbed, for when he went to a new place he did not like to be interfered with when he made his first explorations, and he always preferred making them at night, and alone. You will no doubt think that he could not explore much, tied to a short rope, but if you think the rope made any difference you do not know the ways of an educated goat, and Billy had no Kindergarten education either, but a regular High School training in that respect.

He turned, and taking the rope in his mouth as he had done many times before, he quietly and peacefully chewed it until it fell apart, and then with a kick of his heels, and a wink at the house, he went toward the garden. From this direction the evening breeze was wafting to his nostrils sweet odors of dew-sprinkled lettuce and tender beet tops.

He ate up all the lettuce, or at least all the choice heads, and what beets he did not eat, he stepped on. Then he walked across the flower beds, and trampled down all the flowers, in a short cut to the pump, for he was getting thirsty.

On his way to the pump he thought he saw a man coming down the road, so he hurried along and went up on the veranda of the house to stand in the shadow until the man went by, for he knew that men often interfere with a goat's pleasure, even if it is only a moonlight stroll.

The man having passed, he walked around the veranda trying every now and then to look in at the window to see what kind of a house his new master had. At last he came to the front door and he could not help trying to taste the bell knob, it looked so much like a knob of salt in the moonlight. To be sure he knew that it was not salt, but it did look so good to eat, and he had often eaten things before that were not down on the diet list of a goat, so he took another chew but, horrors! what was that! There was a terrible ringing and clanging in the house,—it sounded like a fire bell; and the next minute Mr. Wagner stuck his head out of the window and wanted to know who was there. Of course there was no answer, and Billy stood as still as possible to listen and see what Mr. Wagner would do next; then he walked to the edge of the porch, and heard Mr. Wagner say, "Who is there? Can't you answer, or are you deaf and dumb, or drunk?"

Still no response, and Billy walked back and gave another lick at the bell, which immediately gave another loud ring. Mr. Wagner drew his head in, and Billy heard him say, "I'll come down and break your stupid head for you, wakening people up this time of the night!" When Billy heard this, he thought that it was time to go, so he scooted around the house, and went and laid down by his rope, just as if he were still tied and had not stirred a peg.

Mr. Wagner opened the door, and finding no one there, walked around the house holding a candle over his head to see if some drunken tramp had not rung the bell. He thought that he heard steps on the veranda as he came to the door, but no one was in sight only Billy Whiskers, apparently asleep by the shed.

"Hello! Billy old fellow, how are you getting along? Seen any-one around here lately?"

But Billy only blinked and laughed in his skin to see Mr. Wagner prancing around in his night-shirt, with the tallow from the candle dropping on his bald head.

Mr. Wagner went in and was about to get into bed, when he thought he saw in the moonlight a figure come out of the shed and go toward the house. The moon went under a cloud just at that minute and was hid from sight, so he kept still, straining his eyes to see and his ears to hear. He heard the chain rattle on the bucket at the well.

"Oh! ho!" he thought, "the tramp thinks that I have gone to bed, and that he will get a drink, and then prowl around some more. Well, we will see. I will just get my shot gun and fire a shot to scare him, if he does not answer."

So grabbing his gun, which always stood by the window loaded for use, he called out again:

"Who is there? Speak, or I'll shoot!"

As the words left his mouth, an object started on a run from the well, and Mr. Wagner fired, not stopping to see what it was, but supposing it to be a man. Just then the moon sailed from under the cloud, and there in the moonlight lay poor Billy Whiskers stunned and nearly frightened to death with a flesh wound in his side. When Mr. Wagner saw what he had done, and that it was only the goat, he pulled down the window, and went to bed, too mad to even go to see if the goat was dead or not.

The next morning Billy was as lively as ever, only a little faint from loss of blood and rather subdued. The children bathed his wound with witch hazel, and after a good breakfast, he was as well as ever, and ready for play or work.

Of course Mrs. Wagner said, "I told you so," several times, only varying it with, "Yes, you just wait and see, that goat will get into more trouble than he is worth, just see if he won't."

When she said this, she did not know of the midnight meal off her nice lettuce he had had in the garden.

Billy did not get into much mischief during the remainder of the day, except chewing up the dish-rags which were hung on the lilac bush to dry, and all the flowers off the oleander.

The next day was his unlucky day, maybe because it was Friday. It happened in this way, Mr. Wagner had some extra nice strawberries, which he had taken special pains to pick and fix up, intending to send them to a friend in town. He told the boys that they could take the goat cart and drive into town, with the berries and some nice lettuce for his friend, and get the mail on the way back.

The boys were delighted at the prospect of driving Billy in the new cart. They packed the things in nicely, and hitching Billy up, drove out of the lane in fine style, on a fast trot. Everything went well until half-way to town, when Jimmy Brown sicked his dog on the goat, and then the trouble commenced.

Billy Whiskers made a plunge for the dog, missed him, but gave the cart a quick jerk, which spilled the boys and the berries out in great shape, and then the scrimmage began. The boys

13

went for Jimmy Brown, and the goat for the dog, dragging the overturned cart with him, and in two minutes, he had sent the dog flying over the fence, with his sharp horns. He then proceeded to walk quietly back to where the strawberries and lettuce were lying in the road, and commenced eating them, as if nothing had happened at all. All this time the boys were pulling each other's hair, and rolling over in the dust, in a regular pitched battle. Billy having eaten all he cared for, walked off and lay down in the shade to rest, still dragging the cart after him. He was just losing himself in sleep, when he was jerked to his feet in a hurry; the cart was straightened; and before he knew what he was about, he was being driven toward home as fast as his legs could go, and from the conversation he learned that they had taken their departure so hurriedly because they had seen Jimmy's big brother coming down the road, and they did not care to stop and fight him too. Arriving at home, with dirty, bloody faces; clothes torn, and no letter of thanks from the people the berries had been sent to, the boys were afraid to go in so they decided that the best plan would be to cry and howl and limp, as if they were nearly dead, to excite their mother's sympathy; so that she would be too frightened to scold them. They made the small holes larger in their clothes, rubbed a little more dirt on their faces, and squeezed a little more blood out of their scratches; and screaming at the top of their voices, they drove into the lane. The ruse was a success, for first came Kate, the cook, to see what was the matter; then John, the hired man; and last mother and father, from out of the garden where they had been examining the damages which Billy had done two nights before.

All mother said was, "That goat has to be sold, Silas Wagner, I told you that trouble would come when you brought that long whiskered animal home."

And the next day the goat was sold.

Billy Whiskers Makes Trouble

THE day after Billy Whiskers was sold to the Biggses he was shut in a small yard to keep him out of mischief. Feeling lonesome, he thought that he would jump the fence and look around a little. He was getting cross-eyed looking through the palings of the fence which were very close together, so suiting the action to the thought, he vaulted over the fence, landing in a kettle of scarlet dye, that had been left there to cool. When he got out of the kettle the fore-part of him was scarlet, and the hind, white, but he did not mind that, so after shaking the drops from his eyes and beard, he was as ready to explore as if nothing had happened.

Seeing the kitchen door open, he went up the steps softly and looked in. He could see no one in the kitchen, and smelling some nice sweet-cakes, which had just been taken out of the oven and placed on the table, he walked cautiously across the floor and began to eat them. From the floor he could only reach a few, so he mounted a chair, and from that stepped onto the table. As he did so, he stepped into a large loaf cake with frosting on it. While kicking that off, and licking the frosting off his feet, he caught sight of a nice red apple that one of the children had put on a small shelf for safe keeping. This he quickly packed away where moth and rust doth not corrupt. Hearing some noise, he was about to get off the table, when raising his head, he faced another goat. But this goat must have come from the infernal regions for in all his life he had never seen such a villainous looking fellow. Billy was no coward, so he backed off as far as the table would allow, and then butted forward as hard as he could. A crash! a bang! and the other goat was upon him, and they both rolled off the table.

17

Where had the other goat disappeared when he had butted him, and what was this thing around his neck? A looking-glass frame, with little pieces of glass sticking in it. Backing out of the frame, Billy went in pursuit of the other goat; for he did not know that it was his own image he had butted in the kitchen looking-glass. Seeing a dark hall-way, he went boldly in, and walked on toward a light he saw at the other end. Arriving there, he found that the light came from a window in the parlor. He marched in, still looking for his rival, but soon forgot him in gazing at the things in the room, especially a fancy basket of fruit under a glass cover. Now Billy was very partial to fruit of all kinds, so he upset the marble-top table the basket was setting on and out rolled all the luscious looking fruit. He bit into a rosy cheeked peach, but of all fruit he had ever eaten, this was the most tasteless and tough. It stuck to his teeth so he could not separate his upper jaw from his lower. Just then he heard voices, and some one say:

"Susie, I heard a terrible crash down stairs. You had better run down and see what it was. You may have left the kitchen door open and the cat possibly came in and upset something."

Then he heard Susie say, "All right, Mum."

18

He thought that if anyone was coming down he had better get out so he started on a run, but the door at the end of the hall had blown shut, and the only other way of escape was up the front stairs. As he reached the top, he saw Susie who had been scrubbing the top of the back stairs, throw down her brush, preparatory to going to see what the noise was. They both caught sight of each other at the same moment, and Susie thought the long, sinister looking, scarlet-bearded face with the horns, that appeared at the top of the stairs, was the devil; and with a blood-curdling scream she threw up her hands and rolled to the foot of the stairs, upsetting the pail of suds that she had clutched when she felt herself falling. There she lay too frightened to move, but Billy rushed on trying to find a way out for he commenced to feel that there would be trouble if he were found.

Mrs. Biggs, hearing Susie scream, rushed to the door with her mouth full of tacks, and a hammer in her hand, just in time to get butted into by Billy, which laid her flat on her back in less time than you can wink. As luck would have it, the shock made her open her mouth and the tacks flew out for if she had swallowed them she would never have gotten off her back.

Billy Whiskers gave her one look when he saw what he had done, and turned and fled back down the stairs, and out the front door between the legs of Mr. Biggs who was just coming in, and Billy being a big goat, and Mr. Biggs a short, stout man, there was not much room to go through, but it was the first daylight Billy had seen, so he gave Mr. Biggs a boost as he straddled his back, which helped him to fall off, over the side of the porch where he landed in a nice soft bed of geraniums.

As Billy was a knowing goat, he decided that they would not care for him after what had happened, nor look for him if he disappeared, so seeing the front gate open, he ran out and trotted down the road and that was the last that was heard of him. His surmises were right. The Biggses never even looked for him.

Billy at the Soda Fountain

AFTER Billy Whiskers had left Mr. Biggs, he trotted slowly down the road wondering where he would get his next meal for he well knew he would never dare go back to Mr. Biggses after upsetting him in the geranium bed and causing all the mischief he had there that day. But being a goat of a cheerful frame of mind and used to looking out for himself, he did not worry much, and decided he would enter the first garden he came to, and make a free lunch off the vegetables, or go into a turnip patch and feast on them for if there was anything he doted on it was nice, sweet turnips, fresh from the fields.

He had gone some distance, and no patch or garden appearing that was not enclosed by a high, barbed-wire fence, he commenced to get discouraged. Feeling hungry and thirsty he was about wishing he had behaved himself at Mr. Biggses so he could go back, when he came to a turn in the road and there before him stood a frame building, with the door open and over the door a large picture of a white Polar bear sitting on a cake of ice, drinking a foaming glass of soda-water, while in a circle round him sat little bears, each with a glass of something cool to drink.

"This is just the place I have been looking for," thought Billy, "where thirsty animals can get a drink." So in he walked, much to the fright of a party of picnickers, who were sitting around a little table drinking soda-water and lemonade, and eating ice-cream.

The man at the soda fountain on seeing Billy was so surprised that he forgot to turn off the fizz he was putting into a glass of soda he was mixing, and it foamed up and ran up his sleeve and all over everything.

This caused the young people to laugh, which made the young man behind the counter mad. He picked up a bottle of ginger-ale and pretended to throw it at Billy, but alas for his intentions! He raised it too high; it hit a large bottle of syrup that stood on a shelf behind him, breaking both bottles at the same time, and instead of hurting Billy, he got a sticky bath of syrup and a shower of ginger in his own eyes. This was adding insult to injury, he thought, and this last mishap turned the laughter of the crowd into a scream of merriment which did not lessen his anger in the least. He grabbed a broom that stood near by and jumping over the counter went for Billy, who all this time had been standing still, looking at the man and waiting for him to give him a drink of some kind.

When Billy saw the man jump over the counter with the broom, he knew he was after him but at the same time he made up his mind that he would not leave that store until he had had a drink of some-thing, — man or no man.

So when the man made a lunge at him with the broom, Billy made a quick rush at the man and planted his head in the middle of the fellow's stomach sending him sprawling on the floor where he landed in the midst of a shower of tooth-brushes he had upset as he flew by the show cases.

This catastrophe frightened the girls and boys who had been sitting sipping soda and laughing at the man, and there was a mad scramble to get out but Billy was too quick for them. He wheeled round and butted the tail end of one fellow's coat so hard that it sent him flying clear through the open door and out into the road where he landed in a mud-puddle.

Then he turned and went for the girls who were all huddled together against the wall, screaming and crying with fright. He walked up to them. As they saw him coming, they thought their time had come and threw up their hands to cover their eyes and screamed harder than ever. But he only took a bunch of green wax grapes off the hat of one of the girls and commenced to chew it, and he would have left them alone but one of the boys who was with them came to their rescue and tried to drive Billy away by giving him a hard blow with a chair he had picked up. This infuriated Billy and he gave the whole bunch of girls a butt and then turned and went for the boy, who was holding the chair high over his head ready to strike. Billy stuck his long horns into the boy's chest and laid him flat on the floor in an instant. Then he walked up on him and planted his two feet on his breast while he lowered his head, licking the boy's face all over with his tongue. This made the boy furious but he could do nothing as the goat was heavy, and with his weight on his chest he thought he would smother.

By that time the soda-fountain man had recovered his breath and came at Billy again with his broom raised ready to strike. Billy saw him coming and left the boy he was standing on, and ran behind one of the tables. Then the chase began; round and round the tables and chairs went the goat with the man after him, upsetting everything as they went, until the store looked as if a cyclone had struck it, with the foaming soda-water and ice-cream running all over the floor.

When Billy thought he had tired the soda man out he ran out the door and sent those that were standing there scattering like a flock of chickens. All you could see for a while were blue stockings, black stockings, white petticoats and heels as the girls ran screaming in all directions. Each girl thought Billy was behind her, but was too afraid to turn round to look, so kept running until she had reached a place of safety, either climbing a fence or getting behind something; and then when she turned to look there was no Billy Goat in sight, for Mr. Billy had disappeared in a small grove behind the store.

25

After Billy had left them he went on through the woods until he came to a little shanty with a small clearing behind it, where cabbages, turnips and such things were planted, and as the gate was open he walked in and began to help himself for he saw at a glance that everything was shut up tight and that there was no one at home.

After eating all he wanted he walked up to the porch where he saw a nice pail of water. This he drank in a twinkle and while doing so thought of that mean soda-water man who would not give him a drink.

"But I don't care," thought Billy, "this tastes better, and I got even with him anyway."

Billy looked round and saw a straw-stack at the further end of the yard and a low shed, which backed up to another shed in the next yard. Billy noticed for the first time that there was another house and yard adjoining the one where he was and from there he could hear voices saying, "Good-night." Then all was still and he walked to the straw-stack and lay down in its shelter and was soon fast asleep.

He had no idea how long he had been asleep when he heard a woman say, in a high-pitched voice:

"Rooney, I told you, you would leave that gate open once

too many times and some one's cow would get in and eat up all the cabbages; and now look, some cow or horse has been in here and eaten and trampled down all of our nice young cabbages and turnips. I've a mind to shake your head off, so I have!"

Then the same voice raised itself and called "Tim, Tim, come here and see what mischief has been done!"

Billy lay still and looked in the direction from which he heard the voice sound, and presently he saw a short, fat, red-headed boy come around the corner of the house. They went to the cabbage patch and began to replant the cabbages that he had trampled down and not eaten, when all of a sudden the woman looked in the direction of the straw-stack and spied Billy.

"Begorry, Tim, what is that? A big white dog or what, down by the straw-stack?" asked Mrs. Rooney.

Tim looked and said: "No, mother, it is a goat. Let's drive him out; he is the one that has done all the mischief," and as he spoke he picked up a stone to throw at Billy.

"Put down that stone and what are ye about, Tim Rooney? Don't ye know a fine Billy goat is a nice thing to have in the family? And it is luck he will bring us by coming to us himself. Put him in the shed, and to-morrow you can hitch him to your cart and make him haul the cabbages to market."

27

Tim pulled up a bunch of nice, fresh carrots and approached Billy. With these he induced Billy to follow him to the shed where he locked him in for the night.

After fastening Billy in, Tim went off and left Billy to take care of himself the best he could, and he soon found a heap of straw which he curled himself upon and was in dreamland in no time.

He had been asleep for several hours when he was awakened by a dog barking at the moon, and he was about going off in another nap when he thought he heard the bleating of a goat in the shed adjoining his.

He pricked up his ears to listen and sure enough he heard it again very distinctly, and at the same time he saw a large knot hole in the board partition that divided his shed from the adjoining one, so he got up and went to look through it to see if he could not see the goat he heard bleating.

Into the next shed the moonlight was streaming, and lying on a pile of straw in the light he saw a beautiful white Nanny goat, that made his old heart palpitate with delight, he was so glad to see one of his own tribe again.

Nanny lay there unconscious of his presence; apparently bleating in her sleep, she lay so still. As she did not move Billy concluded to awaken her so he bleated "Good evening" to her. He had only gotten half through his salutation when she jumped up quickly as if she had been touched with an electric wire, and looking around with a frightened stare, said:

"Good gracious, how you frightened me! Who are you, and where are you, for I see no one?"

"You can't see me, but I am here all the same, at the other side of the shed, looking at you through the knot hole. My name is Billy Whiskers and I come from nowhere in particular and I am bound for the same place. Now, tell me your name and the name of the people you are living with."

"My name is Nanny O'Hara and I live with a family of the same name but I belong to their eldest son, Mike."

"And does he treat you good, my fair friend?" asked Billy.

"Oh, yes," answered Nanny, "as well as boys generally do, but he often makes me pull heavy loads and forgets to feed and water me sometimes."

"Oh, the brute," said Billy, "to make anyone as handsome as you pull heavy loads. How I wish I could help you, for I am strong and used to pulling large loads. The next time he makes you do it just run into a tree and upset his cart, or better still, run away altogether and find someone else to live with."

"Oh, Mr. Billy, I would not dare do either, I am so timid."

"Hark, here comes some one and we must not let them hear us talking," said Billy, "So ta-ta, I'll see you to-morrow."

Sure enough they had heard some one talking. It was Tim Rooney and his chum, Mike O'Hara, whom he was bringing to show his goat. As they unfastened the door, Billy heard Mike say:

"I tell you, Tim, what I will do if he turns out as fine a goat as you say he is. I'll give you a dollar and a half for him."

"So ye'll give me a dollar and a half, will ye? Well I like that—a dollar and a half for the finest goat ye ever laid your two eyes on! Not much—what do ye take me for, an idjet? I don't want er sell but if ye'll offer injucements enough I may think about it, for we have no cart or harness fine enough for so handsome a goat as this one."

"Well, open the door and let's see him," said Mike.

Tim opened the door and there stood Billy Whiskers in all his glory with his most dignified expression mixed with a little disgust, for had he not heard himself valued at *a dollar and a half,*—he that had brought *twenty dollars* in his day!

Tim tied a rope around Billy's neck and led him out of the shed and then the bargaining began again.

"Well, since I have seen him," says Mike, "and find he is pretty large, I'll raise my bid to two dollars cash."

"Not on your life will I sell him for *that*," said Tim.

"Then how does *three* strike you, or you keep your goat for I won't pay another cent. It costs too much to keep a big goat like that; they eat up everything on the place."

This Tim well knew and as he was short of money and a circus was coming to town the next week, he decided to let him go. But not without one last effort to get a little more out of Mike. Now Mike had a hunting knife Tim had long coveted, though it had a rusty blade and a wobbly handle, so he said:

"I'll tell you what I'll do, Mike. I'll let you have him for three dollars cash and your hunting knife with a package of cigarettes thrown in."

"All right, it's a go!" said Mike. So Mike took hold of Billy's rope and led him into his yard and thus Billy changed hands once more and became the property of Mike O'Hara.

Billy Gives the Boys a Ducking in the Mill Pond

 WHEN Mike O'Hara became the possessor of Billy Whiskers he felt as proud as a peacock, for he knew he had made a good bargain and got the best of Tim Rooney for once in his life, and this pleased him mightily as Tim generally got the best of him in a trade.

When he reached his own yard, he called over the fence for Tim to come and see what Billy and Nanny would do when they first saw each other. Tim accepted the invitation with alacrity and jumped over the fence just in time to see Nanny walk out of the shed, as they thought to make the acquaintance of Billy for the first time.

"Now is my chance," thought Billy, "to kiss her, and she can't make a fuss before the boys." So up he walked and kissed her straight on the mouth. Nanny was so surprised that she gave him a startled look, turned her back and walked into the shed again.

"How is that for a cold snub!" said Tim. "Let us harness them together and see what they will do."

"All right," said Mike, "if you will help me make a harness for Billy. I have one for Nanny already."

The two set to work and in an hour had made a harness for Billy out of old leather straps and strings, and then they commenced to harness them to the little cart made out of a packing box set on wheels.

The goats bleated and squirmed, wiggled and bucked, but nothing dismayed the boys and they kept on until the two goats were harnessed up tight and strong to the cart, and then the fun began.

Mike jumped in and took up the reins and Tim followed after, and out of the yard and down the road they went, sending a cloud of dust after them.

From all sides went up the cry: "Look at Mike O'Hara, he has got a new goat!" And from front-yard, back-yard and sand-pile flocked the children to see the fun.

All went well for a quarter of a mile, when Tim, tired of running on behind, jumped in with Mike. Billy felt the additional weight in a minute and he bleated to Nanny that he would be switched if he would pull Tim Rooney, the boy who sold him so cheaply.

"You will have to," said Nanny.

"No, I won't," said Billy. "You just watch and see what I will do! But you must promise to do quickly what I tell you to, or I can't do it, because I am hitched up with you; so, Nanny, you will have to follow me and not pull back."

"All right," said Nanny, "I will do whatever you tell me to."

"Very well. Do you see that pond ahead?"

"Yes," answered Nanny.

"Now go slowly until we get within ten feet of it; then take a long breath and run straight into the water as far as you can go. Don't stop or turn to right or left no matter how hard they pull or scream. Keep right on and we will give Mr. Tim a ducking he won't forget. I'll teach him to stay out of any cart I am pulling!"

They were now ten feet from the pond and Billy gave Nanny the signal call, and with one accord both goats put down their heads and commenced to pull and run for dear life. At first the boys thought it great fun going so fast and neither suspected

IN TWO MINUTES, HE HAD SENT THE DOG FLYING OVER THE FENCE.

See p. 14.

THIS CALLED FORTH A SHOUT OF GLEE FROM THE POLICEMEN WHO WERE
LOOKING OVER THE FENCE.

See p. 60.

what the goats were up to, until Billy gave a quick turn and into the water they went before either boy could jump out.

The water was cold and deep and both boys took hold of the reins to try to stop the goats or make them turn round but to no use; on they went until only the heads of the boys were seen sticking out of the water and both goats were swimming. When they got in Billy enjoyed the wetting he was giving the boys so much, that he did not stop when he had wet their feet, but told Nanny to keep on until they were drenched to the skin.

While they were swimming, Billy said to Nan:

"I am tired of this, beside when we get to shore the boys will pound us for ducking them in the pond, so as soon as we get to shore I am going to run them into a big tree and upset them. This harness is so rotten that it will break at the least strain that is put on it, and when the cart goes over we will both give a big pull which will break it loose from the cart, and then we must run and hide in those thick bushes I see ahead, where the boys can't find us."

"Oh, Billy, I am afraid," said Nanny. "They will surely find us and whip us and shut us up without any supper."

"You're a coward, Nanny. Do what I tell you and I'll take care of you. The boys will never find us if we once get loose and I'll show you where there is the best supper you ever tasted."

And once again Nanny fell in with his plans and both goats began to swim for shore pulling the cart with the two boys still in it, scolding like magpies.

Once on shore, Billy turned to the left, instead of the right which was the way home, and made for a tree that was just the right size to catch the hub of the wheel and overturn the cart in great shape. The boy commenced to switch the goats for the ducking they had given them, and of course, thought the whipping the cause of their rapid progress; but could they have read Billy's mind they would have seen their mistake, for Billy knew the harder and faster he hit the tree the more sure he was of smashing things and getting free.

Smash, bang, roll and tumble! the cart has hit the tree and two boys are rolling over each other in the dust, while two goats go scampering off into the thick bushes that line the road.

Mike recovered himself first and started in hot pursuit of the runaways while Tim sat still on a stone and rubbed his head and nose which was bleeding profusely.

"Hurry, Nanny, hurry," Billy called as he disappeared from sight down a deep ravine. Poor Nanny was so frightened at what she had done, she could not hurry or begin to keep up with Billy, who made great leaps from rock to rock; so she ran under a thorn-apple tree and trusted to its low drooping branches to hide her.

But Mike was too close on her heels. He saw the moving of the branches and knew one of the goats was hiding there. She made a futile attempt to escape but the thorns ran into her so that she gave up and meekly let herself be led back to the cart.

"I have one of them," Mike called out as soon as he came in sight of Tim.

"Which one?" said Tim.

"Nanny," said Mike.

"I'll bet ye it wasn't that old one; he's a foxy old customer, he is, and I'll bet me red shirt ye'll never set your eyes on him again.   Devil take me if I care if ye don't after the wetting and bloody nose he's given me." said Tim.

"You hold Nanny, while I go look for Billy, Tim."

"All right and joy and good luck go with ye, but mark me words ye never will find him when you're looking for him. Better come home with me, and if he ever comes back he'll come back to-night to see Nanny of his own accord," said Tim.   "I know the ways of goats better than ye do."

But Mike did not take Tim's advice.   He went to look for Billy but in about an hour and a half he wished he hadn't, for he saw no signs of the runaway, and came back tired and foot-sore just in time to see Tim and Nanny disappearing over the hill on the way home.

Billy's Adventures in Town

BILLY hid behind some rocks in the bottom of a ravine until he thought the boys had given up looking for him. Then he came out of his hiding-place, and snipped off the fresh young leaves from the bushes as he walked along making up his mind what he would do next.

"It is too bad," he thought, "that Nanny is such a scare-cat and slow runner for if she had only kept up with me she would be free now and we could have a good time here. There are lots of young shoots and juicy leaves for us to eat and plenty of water in the creek to drink.

"Now I must go back and see what has become of her. I expect I will be caught and pounded by the boys, but I told her I would take care of her and as I never break my word, I must go and see what I can do."

He climbed a high hill where he could get a good view of the road and there he saw Tim leading Nanny into Mike's yard, and a mile behind he saw Mike walking slowly along.

"Ho, ho!" said Billy, "they have caught Nan, so there is no use in my trying to get her away now. I will just wait until dark and then go back and butt the shed down and get her out and then we can run away together before they can catch us."

Turning and looking in the opposite direction he saw lying in the valley beneath him a city, and he immediately made up his mind to visit it for it had been a long while since he had been in a large town.

Down the hill he started on a run, loosening stones and pebbles as he went, which rolled after him sending up a cloud of dust.

At the bottom he struck the main road that led to the town, and keeping up his fast gait he was soon within its suburbs.

The first thing he came to was a flower and fruit stand, the owner of which, a greasy, black-looking Italian, was talking to a fat blue-coated policeman. Both stood with their backs turned to the fruit stand.

THE ITALIAN WAS SO HORRIFIED AND DISMAYED TO SEE WHAT HAD HAP-
PENED THAT HE FORGOT WHAT LITTLE ENGLISH HE KNEW.

See p. 41.

THE FARMER STOPPED TO SEE WHAT ALL THE ROW WAS ABOUT.

See p. 122.

Now was Billy's chance. Luscious pears, peaches and grapes lay before him ready to be eaten, and without a moment's hesitation he began to sample each, while now and then he would eat a rose or two between, thus making his own salad. And he found he liked his fruit salad served on rose leaves just as well as on lettuce.

In reaching for an extra delicious-looking pear he had to stand on his hind legs with his fore feet on the lower shelf. But alas, for his greed! His weight on the board that formed the shelf was too much, and it flew up in the air sending the fruit in all directions and making such a racket that the fruit dealer heard it and turned around just in time to see the wreck of his stand.

The Italian was so horrified and dismayed to see what had happened that he forgot what little English he knew and chattered and swore in Italian until you would have thought a dozen parrots had been suddenly let loose.

The policeman tried to stop and catch Billy by spreading out his legs and waving his arms, but Billy only lowered his head and ran between the policeman's legs, upsetting him as he went through for Billy was fat and the policeman short-legged and there was not room to slide through without upsetting the man.

The policeman picked himself up and started in hot pursuit, swearing under his breath that if he ever caught that goat he would club its brains out.

Of course the policeman could not catch up to the fleet-footed Billy, so he called out—"Catch him!" But no one cared to attempt it, especially when Billy lowered his head with the long horns on it and ran at him.

But at last, after dodging in and out of the people on the sidewalk and the carts and wagons in the street, one man was brave enough to try to catch him. He was a big German butcher and he stood plum in Billy's way, and when Billy lowered his head at him, as he had at the others, the butcher caught hold of his horns and gave his neck a quick twist. This made Billy furious and he reared on his hind legs and struck at the butcher with his fore ones, and then the fight began; first one was on top, then the other, and they rolled over and over into the mud

42

of the street, while a big crowd gathered, which cheered and called out:

"I bet on the goat!"

"Give it to him, Dutchie!" and all such expressions, until at last Billy got on his feet again, and with a parting hook he slit the butcher's coat up the back and left him lying in the mud, while he ran off as fast as his legs would carry him. And it is needless to say that none of that crowd tried to stop him.

He had gone through many streets and turned many corners, when he found himself opposite a beautiful, green, cool-looking park.

"This is the place for me," thought Billy, "it looks nice and quiet and as I am tired I will go in and lie down under one of the trees and eat a little grass."

After taking a nice rest and nap under the trees, he awoke, and feeling thirsty thought he would go and quench his thirst at a sparkling fountain he saw before him. He was quietly drinking and every once in a while swallowing a goldfish that swam too near his mouth, when someone from behind gave him a hard hit with a rake.

"It is a pity a goat can't take a drink without being pounded," thought Billy. "But as I have had enough I guess I will move on for I don't like the looks of this man's face, and I know he will give me no peace."

So he walked away slowly, just as if he were going away of his own accord, when the man gave him another hit with the rake. This was too much for Billy's pie-crust temper; he turned on the man, who was gardener of the park, and sent him sprawling over a hay-cock before he knew what had struck him.

As Billy walked toward the high iron fence that encircled the park he saw a policeman coming in at the gate. Now if there was one thing Billy detested, it was a policeman, and he made for him running at full speed with head down, and before the policeman had even seen the goat he found himself hanging by the seat of his trousers to the sharp iron pickets of the fence. Billy left him there struggling, kicking, swearing and calling for help while he made off as fast as his legs would carry him.

Billy Has a Ride in the Police Patrol Wagon

AFTER Billy left the policeman hanging on the fence, he walked through street after street trying to find his way out of the town, so he could go back to Nanny, but the more he looked for the scattered houses of the suburbs, the more closely they seemed to be built, and he found himself on a street where there were nothing but stores and flats. It was beginning to get dark and he was getting hungry and tired.

"I'll turn down the next alley I come to and see if I can't find someone's back gate open where I can go in and rest," thought Billy. He soon found the back yard to a flat and as he stood in the open gate looking up, he could see by the gas light in the different apartments, the cooks getting supper, and could smell the sweet odor, to him, of boiled cabbage.

"Now is my chance," he thought, "to get supper and then come back and sleep in this coal shed I see in the corner."

As there were long flights of stairs that connected one flat with the other, he thought he would commence at the bottom flight and go to the top, stopping at each flat as he went and picking up anything he saw fit to eat. At the first landing, the cook had just been out to the ice-chest to get something for supper and had neglected to shut the door tightly, consequently it was an easy matter for Billy to push it open with his nose, and then help himself to the nice, crisp, fresh lettuce and radishes he saw lying on the shelf. These he ate in a twinkling; next he found a basket of eggs, these he did not care for, but he did want the bunch of large carrots back of the basket, so he stuck his head farther into the chest to reach the carrots and in doing so, his horns ran through the handle of the basket and when he brought his head out of the chest, the basket of eggs came too.

It slipped down until it hit his forehead and then it turned over, spilling the eggs on the floor and making a terrible mess. As the eggs broke, each one made a noise like a small paper

46

torpedo, and Billy knew the noise would bring the cook, so he scooted up the stairs to the next landing, where he kept very still in order to hear what the cook would say when she saw the broken eggs for he heard her coming out.

"Goodness, gracious, me! The grocery boy has dropped a package of eggs on his way up stairs. No he hasn't either, for my ice-box door is open and someone has been stealing my things!" he heard her say, and she hurried down stairs to look for the janitor to tell him that sneak thieves had been at her ice chest.

When Billy heard her go down the stairs for the janitor, he went to the upper flat, for fear the janitor would find him if he stayed where he was. Arriving at the upper flat, he saw a line of nicely-starched, fine linen things,—a baby's cap, two or three handkerchiefs and a lace tidy. These he chewed up and swallowed for he liked the taste of starch and they felt quite like chewing gum in his mouth as he ate them. Then he saw a pan of apples setting outside the door and he ate some of those. While eating he heard the electric bell in the kitchen ring, which scared the life out of him at first, but when he looked in the window and found out what it was, he got over his fright. When the girl left the kitchen to answer the bell,

Billy thought he would go in and take a drink from a pan of milk he saw setting on the table. He had nearly finished the milk and his whiskers were all wet from being in the pan, when he heard a scream and, looking up, he saw the girl standing in the doorway, screaming: "Fire! police! murder!"

"What a goose that girl is," thought Billy, "to make such a racket, she will have the patrol here and four or five policemen if she don't shut up. Guess I will run into her and butt her through the hall and down the front stairs."

Suiting the action to the thought, he started for her but she fled down the hall and ran into a room closing the door after her. As she closed that door, the janitor opened the front door which was directly opposite and Billy getting there just at that time gave the janitor the butt instead of the girl and sent him sprawling on the hall floor.

Before he could get up, Billy ran back through the hall to escape down the back stairs and as he ran he could hear the girl calling: "Fire! police! murder!" out of the window at the top of her voice.

Billy hurried down the outside stairs as fast as he could, but there were so many turns they made him dizzy and as he reached the last flight, he heard the janitor above him call

to someone in the yard not to let that confounded goat escape through the back gate.

Billy laughed to himself, "I would like to see anyone stop me," when all unexpectedly, someone hit him on the head with a club as he made the last turn in the stairs and there before him were three policemen in a line stopping his way out. He butted and kicked and balked, but to no use; they clubbed him until he was almost senseless and then slipped a rope around his neck and dragged him to the patrol wagon that was waiting outside the gate, and with many boosts and pushes they at last succeeded in getting him into the wagon.

As they drove down the street at break-neck speed, Billy vowed to himself that if he ever got away from the police, that he would go back and butt that girl into the middle of next week for screaming, "Fire! police! murder!" until she had brought the patrol wagon.

Billy Joins the Fire Patrol

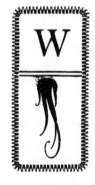

WHEN they arrived at the police station Billy was made to jump out and was led through the station into the back yard, and here he was turned loose. He had been there about half an hour, when he heard a terrible stamping of horses' feet and many bells ringing in the building on the other side of the fence.

Wondering what the racket could be about, he climbed on top of a pile of boxes that were next to the fence and looked into the yard beyond. He found that the building was used as a fire-engine station, and that the racket he had heard was caused by the horses taking their places at the engine ready to start to a fire.

Through two large doors that opened into the yard Billy could see what was going on inside. And when he saw the men jump to their places on the engine and the driver whip up his horses, he became so excited he could stand it no longer and he determined to go with them to the fire. With a spring he was over the fence and following after the engine at a stiff run.

It was a good thing Billy had a strong pair of lungs or he would never have been able to keep up with the fast speed of the fire-engine horses, but he did and arrived at the fire in good shape.

The fire was found to be in a three-story frame house, and when they got there the flames were already coming out of the upper windows; but the strangest thing about the fire was that the inhabitants of the house, if there were any, seemed to be in utter oblivion that their house was on fire for not a person was in sight about the place and all the doors and windows were securely locked.

Two men ran up the steps with axes, while two followed dragging the hose after them. The men with the axes had given one knock to the door when Billy saw what they were up to, and as he had often used his head as a battering-ram, he ran up the steps, and before the men knew he was there, he gave the door a mighty butt with his head which made it crash in and the men and goat fell through the opening.

This tickled the crowd who had gathered to see the fire, and they called out: "Bravo for the goat!"

Billy followed the firemen upstairs but when he got there the smoke was so thick he could see nothing, and it made his eyes smart beside choking him dreadfully, so he decided to go out again. He turned to find the head of the stairs he had come up, but instead of discovering them he ran into the wall and the more he tried to find his way out, the more confused he became. He fell over something and when he regained his feet, after having nearly gone head over heels into a box, as he thought, but which was a baby's cradle, he felt something heavy hanging to his horns. At the same time he heard a baby cry.

"Poor little thing," thought Billy, "everyone has gone out of the house and left the baby asleep and now it is going to be burned to death. Wish I knew where it was; it sounds near but I can't see for this smoke." Just then a little bare foot slipped down over Billy's eyes and then he knew the heavy thing hanging to his horns was the baby.

As soon as he found this out, he tried harder than ever

to find the stairs and presently he found them, and with the baby's clothes still twisted around his horns he **ran** down and out into the street, just in time to meet the baby's nurse coming from the drug-store around the corner. She was wild with joy when she saw the baby and rushed up to Billy to un-fasten the baby's clothes from his horns.

The child was unhurt, and a crowd soon gathered around Billy to pet and praise him for saving the baby's life.

BILLY JOINS THE FIRE PATROL

Billy stayed there until the fire was put out and watched the hose being rolled up, while the firemen that were doing it talked to him all the time.

When the hose was all on the cart and the firemen stepped up on the little step that is at the back to ride home, Billy walked over and stepped up also but he had to stand on his hind legs with his fore feet on the coil of hose in front of him.

One fireman thought this a very clever thing for a goat to do, so he put his arm around his neck and said, "All right, old fellow, you shall ride home with me, but take care for we are going to start and the road is rough and you may fall off." And in this way Billy rode back to the fire station, causing many smiles from the people they passed.

As they drove into the station one of the policemen who was standing outside their station called out, "Where did you get that goat?" Billy's friend called back: "I don't know where he came from; all I know is that he followed us to the fire, where he made himself useful by saving a life."

"Well, we have his brother in our back yard. If not his brother, then one that looks precisely like him."

"Oh, I guess not," answered Billy's friend, "for there are not two such fine looking goats in town."

"Well, I'll show you, come over and see for yourself."

So the two men went into the police station yard with Billy lagging at their heels, laughing to himself to think how fooled the policeman was going to be at not finding any goat there.

When they got to the yard the policeman looked everywhere, but could find no sign of a goat, so went into the station to ask the other policemen where the goat had gone, but none had seen him and all thought he was still in the yard.

"Well that must be my goat, then," said the policeman.

"Not much!" answered the fireman. "You will have to bring better proof than that before I give him up."

"Well, I don't want him anyway," said the policeman, "and you will be glad to get rid of him yourself in a day or two for he is the most troublesome goat you ever heard of. You should hear of the mischief he got into at the flat we took him from."

"Very well," said the fireman, "I'll stand all the trouble he will cause."

And with that he led Billy out of the yard into their back yard and gave him a nice place to sleep, a big dinner and a bucket of water, all of which Billy was thankful for as he was both hungry and thirsty after his trip to the fire.

BILLY JOINS THE FIRE PATROL

After his first ride on the hose-cart, Billy liked it so much that every time the cart went out Billy went too and rode, as he had before, with his hind legs on the step and his fore feet on the coil of hose in front of him and the fireman always steadied him with his arm. And soon this fire company was known as the White Goat Company, with Billy as its mascot.

Billy had been with the firemen about a month, when one day he heard them talking about a procession they were going to be in, that all the fire-engines, hose-carts and hook-and-ladder companies were to be in the parade and that the horses were to have their hoofs gilded and wear collars of roses, and that he, Billy, was to have his horns and hoofs gilded also, and wear a rose collar and be led by a chain made of roses, by one of the firemen who was to wear a red shirt, black trousers and high patent leather boots and his fireman's hat with a visor.

When Billy heard this he said, "I won't march in their old procession, and make a circus of myself. I'll run away first." But he did not get a chance.

When the morning of the day of the procession came, Billy watched the firemen polish the brass of the engine and trim it with garlands of flowers tied with bright colored ribbons; but when they commenced to gild the horses' hoofs one of them said to him:

"It will be your turn next Billy; we are going to give you a scrubbing in the tub until your hair is as soft and shiny as silk, and then we are going to gild your long horns and tie blue ribbons on them, and put the handsomest wreath of pink roses we can find round your neck. My! but you will look fine, Billy. And we expect you to behave and walk in a dignified manner, for the Fire Marshal is going to give you a gold medal to wear round your neck for saving the baby's life."

"It is very nice of them to give me a medal," thought Billy, "and they have been good to me; but I don't like being scrubbed and dressed up like a clown, beside I am getting tired of town life and I long for the country and Nanny. I might as well run away one time as another, so I will watch my chance, and when they are all busy and not looking, I will walk out of the station quietly, as if I were only going for my usual walk up the street, and when I get to the corner, I will turn it and once out of sight I will run until I get so far away they can't find me."

But for once Master Billy's plans were foiled for just as he was walking out of the station one of the firemen saw him and said:

BILLY JOINS THE FIRE PATROL

"Here, here, Billy, **not so fast!** We are ready for you now and if you go for a walk there is no knowing when you will come back."

And he took Billy by the horns and led him into the back yard where another fireman had a big tub of soapy water ready to put him in.

Billy stood in the tub and submitted to the scrubbing until the soapy water ran into his eyes and then he got mad and butted the fireman, who was holding his horns, clear over, and kicked the other man, who was scrubbing him, in the stomach; and then around and around the yard he ran bleating and shaking his head, wild with the smart of the soap that was in his eyes.

"Here, Jack, this will never do," said one fireman to the other, "he is not half clean. Let us get the hose and turn it on him while he is running around."

"All right," said the other, "that will be great sport."

And they got the hose and soon they were squirting it over Billy as he ran, first on one side and then on the other, and no matter where he went the stream of water followed him and played all over him, and if he stopped running and hugged the fence it was worse than ever for then the water flowed in a perfect stream and doused him from head to foot, sending a spray over the fence.

All the firemen had come out to see the fun and when the policemen in the next yard heard a great deal of laughing and racket in the fireman's back yard, they too hurried to the fence and watched the fun.

Of course, this only added to Billy's rage, to see his hated enemies, the policemen, laughing at him, and he vowed he would get even with them some day, and with the firemen right away, for he knew his strength. With a bound and a quick run he made for the group of firemen that were tormenting him and butted and hooked them in all directions, and sent the fireman who was playing the hose on him sprawling into the tub of soapy water that but a few minutes before he had Billy in.

This called forth a shout of glee from the policemen who were looking over the fence, and with another angry bound Billy went for them and butted the fence down that they were leaning against, and they made their escape into the police station just in time, for Billy came through the fence and after them, right up to the door they had run through.

He gave it one butt and then turned and walked back into his own yard where he lay down on a pile of straw to cool off after his exertion. He had been there about half an hour when his pet fireman came out with a large plate in his hand heaped full of good things to eat and as he walked toward Billy, the goat could smell the cabbage, turnips, apples and carrots. He bleated a friendly greeting to let the fireman know that he would not hook him if he came nearer and the man came up and set the plate down under Billy's nose and Billy gave him a goat smile showing that all was forgiven and began to eat.

While he was eating this same fireman went in and brought out a kettle with a brush in it and began to gild Billy's horns and hoofs. Then he tied a wreath of roses round his neck and went to get the rope wound with roses to lead him by. But while he was gone Billy ate up the front of the wreath and as much more of it as he could reach.

When the fireman came back dressed for the parade with the rose chain in his hand that he was to lead Billy with, he spied the eaten wreath, and said:

"Why, Billy, you beat any bad boy I ever heard of for mischief! Now you will have to come into the station and have another wreath tied round your neck, and I bet you won't chew this one for I will tie it so close to your neck you can't reach it with your mouth."

As they went in the station Billy heard a band playing and the rat-ta-tah-tah of the drums, and when they heard the music the engine horses, all decked in rose collars and bridles, with plumes on their heads, started to prance and pull the beautifully draped and polished engine out of the station to join the procession.

And before Billy knew what was up, he was led out and made to march in the procession between the engine and hose-cart. After they had started he rather enjoyed it for from all sides he heard the people say:

"There, look! There goes the goat that saved the baby's life."

"Isn't he a beauty?"

"See what nice, white, silky hair he has!"

"Yes," Billy thought, "if they could have seen the firemen scrubbing me, I expect they would have laughed like the policemen did." But it all tickled his vanity for Billy was as conceited a goat as you could well find.

They had been marching for some time and Billy was getting tired of the slow gait and being made to stay between the engine and hose-cart instead of riding on the hose-cart as he had been in the habit of doing, when he heard the plaintive bleat of a goat and the sound of a whip.

BILLY JOINS THE FIRE PATROL

"My!" thought Billy, "how that voice reminds me of Nanny."

Just then a little cart, with a can of milk in it, drawn by a goat came in sight around the corner, and who should be pulling it but Nanny, with the big, clumsy Mike Rooney cracking the whip at her and every once in a while giving her a stinging cut which had caused Nanny to cry out as Billy had heard.

Mike had just given Nanny another and an extra hard cut with the whip, when Billy recognized Nanny and with a bound he was at her side leaving the fireman behind him and upsetting Mike in his mad haste to get to Nanny.

When Mike regained his feet he came at Billy with the butt of his whip raised to strike him, but before he did so, he recognized Billy as his long-lost goat, and was going to make up with him and hitch him to the cart to help Nanny draw it, when Billy made a plunge at him and sent him sprawling into the street. Then he butted the cart over and spilled the milk and told Nanny to turn around and run toward home and he would keep Mike off.

Nanny did as she was told and soon the harness broke and let her loose from the overturned cart. By this time Mike was on his feet again, furious and mad enough at Billy to kill him had he caught him, but with a kick of his heels in the air Billy and Nanny had left him and were running away as fast as they could while the firemen and the crowd stood still and watched.

Mike ran until he was all out of breath and in turning a corner sharply he ran into another boy coming in the opposite direction. This made the boy mad and he struck at Mike hitting him in the jaw. That was too much for Mike who was already angry at being outwitted by the goats, so he pitched into the boy and they fought until both had black eyes and bloody noses and a policeman coming up at that time arrested them both for disorderly conduct. While all this was happening the goats had made good their escape.

Billy and Nanny Get into Mischief

WHEN next we see Billy, he and Nanny are lying peacefully in the moonlight fast asleep. After running away from Mike, Nanny showed Billy the way into the country, for she knew the road well, as she had had to draw a can of milk to town every morning.

When they were once out of town Billy said:

"Now, Nanny, we must find a nice meadow somewhere in which we can get some grass to eat and water to drink and then you must tell me all that has happened since last I saw you. But first we must get as far away from the road Mike will have to take to get home as we can, or he will find us."

So they turned off at the first cross-road they came to

and hurried on until they found the fine, green pasture where we now see them.

The next day they were in this same pasture enjoying themselves when they saw some boys coming toward them. At first they thought the boys were looking for them; but soon discovered from their conversation that the boys were going swimming in a little lake at the end of the meadow near the woods. They passed close by the goats without paying any attention to them

One boy had a bag of pop-corn he was eating and Billy smelling it commenced to long for some. The firemen had bought salted and buttered pop-corn for him every day, and the smell of this made him hungry and he determined to get the bag from the boy.

"But how can you, Billy?" asked Nanny, when he told her he was going to get the pop-corn.

"I'll tell you; when they leave their clothes on the bank and go in swimming I will steal up and eat what is left in the bag, and anything else I find in their pockets."

"How are you going to get anything out of their pockets without hands?"

"Why, I will eat pocket and all if I smell anything in there I like," answered Billy.

BILLY AND NANNY GET INTO MISCHIEF

"Billy Whiskers, you are the most determined goat I ever heard of," said Nanny. "If you want anything you are going to have it, no matter how you have to get it."

"I guess you are right, Nan. But if you had ever tasted salted and buttered pop-corn you, too, would have it if you had to hook all five of those boys into the lake to get it. Come along, and we will go over near the lake so when they go into the water we can go through their clothes and I will give you your first taste of a town delicacy in the shape of pop-corn."

Billy and Nanny soon arrived at the bank of the lake where the boys had gone in swimming, and behind a clump of bushes they found the boys' clothes.

Billy lost no time in smelling out the bag of pop-corn but alas! when found, it was empty. Billy's disappointment knew no bounds and he began to vent his spleen on the clothes that were lying around by hooking and stamping on them. When throwing a coat up in the air on his horns two nice red apples rolled out of one of the pockets. After eating one of these and allowing Nanny to eat the other, he felt a little less angry and commenced to smell around for something else equally as good.

All this time they could hear the boys shouting and splashing in the water, oblivious of the mischief that was being done to their clothes, for they could not see the goats through the bushes.

"Oh, Billy, come here!" called Nanny, "and see what I have found. It smells awfully good but I don't know what it can be."

Billy went and after smelling the coat pronounced the good smell to come from a piece of gingerbread in one of the pockets.

"How do you know?" asked Nanny.

"Well, I guess if you had eaten as many pieces of gingerbread as I have you would not forget the name. When I lived at Mr. Wagner's, his boys used to give it to me often."

But the trouble was to get it out of the pocket now that it was found. Billy threw the coat up in the air, shook it in his mouth and did everything else he could think of, but the gingerbread would not fall out, so when the coat turned wrong side out and the pocket lay exposed he ate pocket and all, forgetting to save any for Nanny.

"Oh, Nanny, forgive me, I forgot to give you some and you found it, but don't care for it did not taste very good and I felt something hard go down my throat and I think I must have swallowed a jack-knife also.

BILLY AND NANNY GET INTO MISCHIEF

"Here is something good, Nanny. A white shirt with starched cuffs. You take one sleeve and I will take the other and I know you will like the starchy taste."

The goats were standing there each chewing on a cuff when they heard the boys coming and it happened that they both heard the noise at the same time, but turned to run in opposite directions which tore the shirt from top to bottom and when the boys first saw the goats they were scampering off with a piece of shirt waving from their mouths.

The boys started after them but the rough ground the goats were running over hurt the boys' feet so they had to give up and content themselves with throwing stones at the two runaways.

When the boys went to see what damage had been done they found one boy minus a pair of trousers, another a shirt and all the rest had lost their collars and cuffs to say nothing of the pockets that were missing.

But the boy whose trousers were gone was in the worst fix, as the others could go home without any collars and the boy minus a shirt could button his coat up tight to his neck and no one would know he had no shirt on. But alas for the trouserless boy! What was he to do? At last they hit on a plan. He was to take one of the boys' coats and stick his legs in the sleeves and button the coat tightly in front and tie it on round his waist with a string. This he did, but when he had to walk he could only take the very shortest of steps. This, with the comical picture he made, sent the boys into peals of laughter, and they rolled on the ground and held their sides for pain from laughing when he stubbed his toe and fell head over heels, or when he tried to climb a fence.

Billy and Nanny Are Married

AFTER leaving the boys the two goats trotted on and soon came out on the other side of the wood and saw before them a beautiful valley. Grazing peacefully beside a little brook that ran through it, they saw a herd of goats. And at the upper end of the valley beyond them they saw a large old-fashioned farmhouse with its stables and outhouses.

"Nan, let us go down and introduce ourselves to the head goat of the flock and see if they won't let us stay with them for awhile. There are so many of them that the farmer won't notice us among them when he drives them into the stable to-night, and it will be a good place for us to stay until Mike stops hunting for us, for I know he won't give us up in a hurry and is probably looking for us now, and I don't propose to live with such a common family as Mike belongs to, for until now I have only lived with first-class families."

Nanny agreed to join the goats so the two trotted down the hill bleating as they ran to attract the attention of the other goats. The goats soon heard them, stopped eating and looked up, and when Billy and Nanny were within speaking distance the leader of the goats, a large black fellow, walked out to meet them.

Billy introduced himself and then Nanny to the old goat who in return told them his name was Satan and that he would be glad to have them join his flock, adding that he was always glad to get ahead of boys, as he had received some rough usage at their hands when younger.

"If we see Mike coming after you, we will all form in a circle around you and Miss Nanny so he can't see you."

All that day Billy and Nanny stayed with the other goats who never tired of hearing the new-comers tell of the adventures they had had, some of which seemed impossible to those country goats who had never been off their own farm.

That evening when the farmer drove the goats home he did not notice Billy and Nan until he had got them into the little enclosure where he always drove them to be fed; but when he stood by the fence with his arm on the upper rail counting them, his eye detected Billy immediately as he was so much taller than any of the other goats, even old Satan, the leader.

"Ho, Ho!" he thought to himself, "where did this fine goat come from, I wonder," and when he went to drive Billy apart to get a good look at him he spied Nanny who was trying to hide behind Billy.

"So my fine goat, you have brought your mate with you?" And Billy who was not afraid of any man or thing, bleated back that he had, though I doubt whether the man understood him or not.

The man walked round and round Billy taking in all his fine points and talking to himself all the time, but when he saw the gilt shining on Billy's horns he stopped and stared in astonishment. Then he slapped his knee with his hand and said: "Well, I swan! I bet that goat has run away from the circus that is in town for I don't know how else he got his horns gilded."

Everything went smooth as silk for three nights but on the fourth, had you been looking you would have seen an unusual commotion among the goats when they were turned loose after milking time to graze in the meadow during the night, as they were allowed to do when the weather was fine; and to-night was an ideal night with a low hungry moon that lit up everything as bright as day.

I know you are anxious to hear what the commotion was all about, so will tell you. Billy and Nanny were to be married by the old parson goat of the flock, and then they were all going to break through the neighbor's fence into his turnip patch and eat up all his turnips.

It is needless to say that this scheme originated in Billy's head, though from Satan's name you would have imagined it more likely to have come from him; but in reality that goat was as meek as a lamb and Satan should have been Billy's name by rights for in his heart he was as mischievous as Satan.

The wedding went off beautifully and the groom, minister and all the others kissed the bride and you never saw a sweeter one than poor little meek Nanny with her gentle ways; and to think she was going to marry a goat twice her size and as fiery tempered as she was mild! But people frequently marry their opposites, and why should not goats?

After the wedding they all ran skipping and jumping over to the turnip patch and when they got there Billy, Satan and two other old goats threw their weight against the fence and with a crash it caved in and the whole flock of goats climbed over the broken rails into the field where they feasted until daylight.

The farmer who owned the field happened to look out of his window next morning while dressing and saw the goats. He hurried into his boots, and hatless and coatless, started out of the house calling to his dogs to follow him.

And the first thing the flock knew, several dogs were barking and biting at their heels. Billy kept close to Nan and when a dog came up to them he hooked him howling up into the air. Soon the goats were all on their side of the fence again and the neighbor was fixing up his fence as best he could, scolding all the time he did so, saying:

"I'll sue Farmer Windlass for the damage his pesky goats have done, so I will, for the hateful things have eaten up all my turnips, tops and all!"

Several days after this when the goats were all in the meadow, and Nanny was lying down under a tree for a nap, Billy, who was tired of the monotony of going day after day to the same place, stole off and went up to the house to see what amusement he could find.

When nearly there he came to a white-washed rail fence that separated the pasture from the lane that led to the house. This he went over easily by taking it at a running jump. Then he followed the lane until he came to the house, the yard of which was separated from the lane by a picket fence; but as good luck would have it the gate was open, so Billy walked in and went around to the kitchen door for he heard voices in the parlor, which is an unusual thing in the country as they generally entertain their company in the sitting room. Immediately Billy knew they must have company for dinner.

"I'm lucky," thought Billy, "I have come just in time to get something good to eat, but I must be careful and not let them see me or they will drive me back to the pasture. I will walk on the grass so my hoofs won't make any noise and listen under the window, and when the cook leaves the kitchen I will go in and steal something good."

While standing under the window with his head cocked to one side listening, he noticed that the outside cellar doors were open. He started to go down cellar and see what he could find, for he knew they would put all their good things in the cellar until time to bring them up to the table.

Tiptoeing his way along, he sneaked down the cellar stairs and there before him on a table were twelve plates of salad all garnished and ready to be served. The salad was delicious as it was cool and crisp and made of chicken served on young lettuce leaves garnished with radishes. It was so palatable he ate it all up even licking the plates; he had never been told it was bad manners to lick your plate.

Then he saw a floating-island pudding, with the whites of eggs heaped up high and dotted with candied cherries, floating on the custard underneath. He ate part of this, getting his head covered with eggs. Next he spied several cakes covered with icing which he licked off. Next he saw an ice-cream freezer. Now he had never seen an ice-cream freezer before so he thought it must contain something good if he could only get the top off to see what was inside. In trying to get it off he upset the whole thing and as the ice rattled out on the floor making a terrible noise, he left everything and ran for the cellar door just in time to escape the cook who had heard the noise and had come down the inside stairs to see what was the matter.

Billy ran around the house and seeing the front door open and no one around, as they were all in the dining room, he went in and up stairs. Here he nosed around smelling things and upsetting things generally, when he came to the bed where the ladies had laid their wraps. On one of the hats he saw a bunch of green leaves; of course, he thought them real until he tried to eat them and the wire stems were in his mouth. Then he tried to eat a beautiful red rose on another hat with no better success so he left them, and was just leaving the room when he saw another goat coming in. He stopped to look at the goat and the other goat stopped to look back. Then he lowered his horns and shook his head, which the other goat did also. Now it made Billy mad to have a goat mock everything he did, so he bleated for him to stop immediately or he would hook him down the front stair. The other goat opened his mouth to bleat but no sound came from it and Billy stared at the new-comer harder than ever but the stranger goat only stared back. Then Billy bleated, "You get out of here in double quick time or I will have a fight with you!" The goat opened its mouth as before but no sound came from it and it continued to stand in Billy's way and stare right in his face.

This was too much for Billy. He had given him warning to get out of the way and he would not, so now he was going to make him, and he went for the goat intending to butt him out of the door. But instead of his head feeling the soft side of the goat he hit something hard which broke in a thousand pieces cutting his head and making the blood flow down his face. When this happened Billy knew he had been fooled and had butted his own image in a mirror and that there had been no goat there.

The crash brought the ladies from the dining room headed by Mrs. Windlass but when they got to the foot of the stairs to come up, they saw a large white goat standing at the top with blood flowing down his whiskers. The sight of the blood as much as the goat made one lady faint and all the others ran in different directions while Billy scampered down and out of the house.

He was making for the pasture again as fast as he could when he met a big turkey cock which spread his tail and swelled himself out intending to keep Billy from passing, but when Billy came up to him he quietly hooked him on top of the shed where he left him with all the pride knocked out of him and his feathers drooping.

Billy kept right on and was soon in the pasture. When Nanny saw her Billy all bloody she commenced to cry and wanted to know who had shot him. Billy told her he had not been shot and that he had only cut his head a little on a piece of broken glass. This explanation satisfied Nanny and she asked no questions. Naturally Billy did not explain how he had hooked his own image.

Billy walked over to the little stream that flowed through the pasture and let the water run over his head and face and soon all trace of blood was washed away, and when the farmer looked them over that night to find the goat with the bloody face, that his wife had told him had done all the mischief, he could find none, so he took it for granted that some stray goat had come in and done all the damage, and once again Billy got off without being punished for his misdeeds.

Billy As a Performer in the Circus

ONE day when all the goats were grazing in the pasture, Billy looked up and saw coming toward them the farmer and a large, fat man.

"What can they want?" thought Billy. "I guess I will walk out and meet them and hear what they are talking about."

As he came within hearing distance, he heard the farmer say: "Here he comes now, the one I was telling you about and I don't think you will have any trouble in teaching him anything you want to, for he seems very smart and not afraid of 'Old Nick' himself."

"That is good," said the circus-man, "for a timid goat is no good in a circus where they have to be with all the other animals."

"So," thought Billy, "this is a man from the circus up in town and he is thinking of buying me and making me perform in his circus. Well, I guess not," and he kicked up his heels in their faces and skipped off to the other side of the stream where they could not get him.

"It takes three to make a bargain where there is a goat in the case," said Billy to himself, "and I will give them a good chase if they try to catch me. And should they catch me, I pity the men and animals at the circus when I get there for I shall use my sharp horns to advantage and split a hole in their old tent and come back to Nanny. Now they are looking at Satan, maybe the man will buy him. No, I am afraid he won't for he is shaking his head and pointing at me and here they come. The farmer is holding out his hand as if he had something in it for me to eat. Oh, no, Mr. Farmer, I am too old a goat to be caught with chaff. However, I will stand still on this side of the stream and see what they will do."

And there Billy stood with his head raised waiting for them and he made as fine a picture of a goat as you ever saw, standing on a little green knoll with the silvery stream running at his feet.

The circus-man was delighted with him for he was almost

twice the size of any other goat he had ever seen, and he thought how fine he would look dressed up as a professor with his long, silky beard.

By this time the men were directly opposite Billy and he noticed that the circus-man kept his hands behind him all the time, but presently he drew them forward and in one he held a rope with a long loop in it.

"So, ho," thought Billy, "he expects to tie that rope around my neck, does he? Well, let him cross the stream and catch me first."

But while Billy was thinking this the circus-man was making the rope fly round and round his head in a long circle, and soon with a quick twist, the rope straightened out and the loop fell over Billy's head and settled on his neck while he stood looking at them.

Billy was the most surprised goat you ever saw, for it was the first time he had ever seen a lasso thrown and had he only known it, the circus-man had been a cowboy in his younger days and lassoed many head of cattle. When Billy found he was fairly caught, his pride had a fall, for he had thought himself too smart to be caught, and instead of him leading the men a chase and making them cross the brook to get him, they were pulling him off the bank and through the water, making him follow them.

At first he tried to pull back and get away, but he had to give that up, for the rope tightened round his neck. and shut off his breath and he was glad enough to follow where they led.

When Nanny saw what had happened she ran up to Billy bleating as if her heart would break for she was very fond of him, and she was afraid they were going to kill him or take him away forever.

"Don't cry, Nanny. I will get loose and come back to-night, or to-morrow night sure, if I can't get loose to-night; so don't take on so. I know my way back and a circus tent is not a hard thing to get out of."

"But, Billy dear, they may tie you as they have now, and then you can't get loose," said Nanny.

"Oh, yes I can, when they leave me alone, I can chew the rope in two."

"But can't I go with you, Billy? I feel so terribly at being left alone and, think of it, we have not been married two weeks."

"What a pretty face that little Nanny goat has," said the circus-man.

"Yes," answered the farmer, "they both came to the pasture one day and joined my goats and have been here ever since. I never knew where they came from, or whom they belonged to."

"Well, here we are at the barn, you must run back, little Nanny; I can't take you with me to-day, though it does seem a shame to separate you two lovers," said the circus-man.

As Billy went through the bars he halted a second to give Nanny a last good-bye kiss; and with the tears streaming down her face, Nanny stood and watched him until they were out of sight.

The circus-man tied Billy to the back of his buggy and whipping up his horse he started for town. Billy had to run fast to keep up and though he got out of breath, he could not stop unless the horse did. The worst of it was the horse kicked up such a dreadful dust that it nearly blinded Billy as it flew up in his face from under the buggy. At last they came to the outskirts of the town, where the circus tents were pitched, and Billy was untied from the buggy and led inside a large tent where cages of wild animals were arranged around the outer edge, while in the center two elephants and four camels were tethered. When he got inside, the circus-man called to one of the men to bring him a strong peg. This he drove into the ground and tethered Billy to it, like all the other animals were fastened. Then he told the man to bring him a bunch of straw for the goat to lie on, and a bundle of hay for him to eat.

"Hay," thought Billy, "after nice tender young grass and turnips! Well, I won't stay here long, that is one sure thing. I wonder if I can understand a word of what these heathen, foreign animals say, but I expect I can read their minds, if I can't understand their tongues for most animals are mind readers and mind is the same the world over, though their thoughts are not the same."

While Billy was thinking this, the circus-man and the other man left the tent and Billy was startled by the elephant sticking his trunk up to Billy's mouth and asking him to speak through it, as he was a little deaf and used his trunk as an ear trumpet. He was just going to introduce himself to the elephant and ask the elephant's name in return, when one of the camels in a weak, weary voice asked the same question he had been going to ask the elephant; so he introduced himself to the camel and she in return presented him to all the other animals that were within hearing distance. She did not introduce him to any of the beasts in the cages, as she said the animals that were loose looked down upon the caged ones and seldom spoke to them. The name of one of the camels was Miss Nancy, and she was a regular old maid of a camel, who did nothing but gossip and ask questions.

"Have you ever performed in a circus or traveled with one before?" she asked Billy. When hearing that he had not, she rolled up her eyes, a habit she had, and exclaimed: "Poor uneducated beast, what you have missed, never to have been taught to perform in a circus." This was a calamity in her eyes. She could not remember ever being anywhere else, as she had been born in a circus in this country shortly after her mother had been brought here from Persia.

"I am so glad I was not born in Persia, for had I been I should have had to carry heavy loads and cross the burning desert with very little water to drink. While now, all I have to do is to march in the processions and then stand and look wise while the boys feed me peanuts as they walk into the circus to see the performance. Oh, you will like being with us when you get used to the confinement," she said.

"For mercy sakes! Nancy, do keep still and give some one else a chance to talk," said her mother.

Just then the lion roared and when he roared, all the other animals stopped talking for he was still looked upon as king of the beasts although he was caged. They all stood a little in awe of him for fear he would break through his cage and chew them up, as he threatened to do so many times when they did not stop talking immediately when he roared.

This time he roared to know who the new comer was and if he was an American relative of his, for as Billy had a beard like the lion's, only much longer, the lion thought he must be an American lion.

"Come over here, near my cage, Mr. Beardy, where I can see you," said the lion.

"I can't," said Billy, "my rope is too short."

"Oh, very well," he roared back, "I will see you in the procession, to-morrow, for I hear you are to march back of my cage."

The lion's keeper came in to see what the lion was roaring about and in passing Billy he stopped to get a good look at him, and presently he was joined by another man, who Billy found out took the part of the clown and who was expected to walk by Billy's side in the procession while a monkey rode his back.

BILLY AS A PERFORMER IN THE CIRCUS

"You are a pretty fine looking goat, old fellow, and I expect we will become great friends. Here is a lump of sugar to begin our friendship with, or do you prefer tobacco?" said the clown.

"He seems like a nice man," thought Billy, "but I never thought to see the day when I would march in a procession with a monkey on my back and a clown at my side, and I don't know whether I will allow him to ride or not, but I guess I will behave for awhile and see what life is like under a circus tent."

The next day dawned bright and fair and there was great commotion throughout the circus, getting ready for the eleven o'clock procession that was to march through the streets. Early in the morning, Billy was led into the sawdust ring, and a peculiar saddle like a little platform was strapped to his back. This the monkey was to dance on, dressed as a ballet girl, with yellow, spangled skirts, a satin bodice and a blue cap with a feather in it on his head.

When Billy first saw the monkey in this dress walking on his hind legs toward him to get on his back, he had a good mind to toss him up to the top of the tent, he felt so disgusted; but his curiosity got the better of him and he decided to wait and see what they expected him to do next. He soon found out. They wanted him to trot around the ring, and not jump when the ring master cracked his long lashed whip at him, while the monkey danced on his back and jumped through paper rings, as the lady circus riders do.

"This is very easy," thought Billy, "I don't mind this in the least, only I don't want to go around too many times one way for it makes me dizzy."

"That will do for this morning, Billy, you are a good goat," said the man. Just then the monkey jumped off Billy's back, and as he ran past him, he gave Billy's beard a pull. Like a shot Billy was after him and had the monkey not run up a pole, Billy would have killed him. From that time on, Billy and the monkey, whose name was Jocko, hated each-other and an outward peace was only kept up when someone was around to keep them apart.

The monkey would climb a pole or sit on top of a wagon, or anything high that was handy, so Billy could not reach him and then call him names and sauce him until Billy pawed the earth with rage, which made the monkey laugh. The only one that could get even with the monkey's tongue was the parrot, and she and the monkey would sit and sauce each other by the hour.

BILLY AS A PERFORMER IN THE CIRCUS

Billy was about cooled down from his fuss with the monkey, when he heard a bugle call and the elephant told him that it was the signal for the procession to start. While Billy had been put through his paces in the circus ring, the elephants had been decked out in scarlet blankets embroidered with gold and funny little summer houses, as Billy thought, strapped to their backs, in which ladies were to ride. The camels had also been fixed up, and from four to six horses, with waving plumes on their heads, had been hitched to each circus wagon.

At another signal from the bugle, they all started to move, led by the men and women performers, dressed in their best spangled velvet suits. Then came what Billy thought to be the best thing in the procession, a golden chariot drawn by twelve Shetland ponies, each pony ridden by a little boy postilion, in scarlet velvet; while in the chariot sat a beautiful, little, golden-haired girl, dressed as a queen, with a diamond crown on her head.

It fairly took Billy's breath away, he thought it all so beautiful, and he started to follow.

"All right, Jim, let him go there if he wants to. He probably thinks the ponies are goats and will behave better than if put with the lions."

"What an idiot that man is!" thought Billy, "to think I don't know a pony from a goat."

It was a good thing they let him march there for he was so taken up with watching the ponies in front of him that he forgot to be mad at Jocko, who was going through all sorts of antics on his back and swinging on Billy's horns. Everything was going smoothly when Billy saw Mike O'Hara coming out of the crowd; he came up to the clown that was walking beside him and said: "Look here, that is my goat!"

"Well, I guess not, you must be crazy."

"I'll prove it to you," said Mike. "Do you see that black spot on his forehead and that he has one black hoof and all the others are white?"

"That don't prove anything," said the clown. "You just noticed that as we were walking along, and now you come up here and try to claim our goat."

"I'll give you another proof," said Mike. "He will come when I call him."

"All right, call him, and I bet he won't follow you," said the clown.

Mike held out his hand and called him by name, but Billy did not turn an inch though he knew he belonged to Mike. He did not propose to go with him and be made to pull milk carts. He preferred to stay where he was as he liked the excitement of a circus life.

When Billy did not go to Mike, it made the clown laugh and he said: "There, I told you so. The goat never saw you before."

"Yes, he has," said Mike, "but it is just like his cussedness to pretend he don't know me."

"Go along, I can't bother talking to you any more," said the clown, as all this time Mike had been walking beside the clown as they marched.

"Well, you need not talk to me any more," said Mike, "but I am going to have my goat." And with that he caught hold of Billy's horns and was going to lead him away.

"Here, take your hands off that goat, you are stopping the procession!" But Mike held on and the clown gave him a hit in the ribs. Mike struck back and a policeman, who was standing in the crowd, ran out and arrested Mike for disorderly conduct and for stopping the procession. This was the second time that Mike had been arrested on Billy's account.

When the procession returned to the tents, all the animals and horses were fed and allowed to rest so as to be fresh for the afternoon's performance. Billy had been resting only a short time, when a couple of men came toward him, one carrying a table and the other a long black gown of some kind.

"What in the world are they going to do now," thought Billy.

When they came up to him, the man that was carrying the table put it down and then brought a high backed arm chair and set it up close to the table. Then the men came up to Billy and one of them said: "Now, old fellow, we are going to make a professor out of you," and with that they both took hold of him and made him stand on his hind legs while they put the black gown on him and a black skull cap on his head, and a pair of spectacles on his nose,—the latter they had to tie on. Then a man got on each side of him and supported him to the table where they made him sit in the chair. They put his forehoofs on the table and a large book before him and a pen behind his ears. When they had him all fixed, you never saw such a wise looking professor in your life as he made, with his long, white beard. The men were so delighted with his appearance and the way he behaved when dressed up, that they called all the rest of the circus people to come and look. Of course they laughed and praised and petted Billy, until he was nearly bursting with conceit and they all agreed that it would tickle the children most to death to see how solemn and straight a goat could sit in a chair.

"Now Billy, we will take these things off and let you rest for your back must be tired as you are not used to sitting up, but you will get used to it and it won't make you tired after awhile. Come here, and I will give you this nice red apple for being such a good goat. You behaved so nicely that I think we will venture to show you off at the performance this afternoon."

This they did and he got more encores and whistles and clapping of hands than anything else that was shown that afternoon, more even than the ponies. Before they brought him in, the Ring Master came in and said: "Now ladies and gentlemen, I am about to introduce to you the oldest and most wonderful astrologer now living. He will read to you, from a mystic book, the fate of the world and whether it is to be destroyed by fire or water."

When he had finished speaking, four men drew a platform in, on which Billy was seated in his chair at the table. But the strangest part of it all was, that when everything was still and the crowd were all watching him, he commenced to read and turn the pages of the book, and he spoke so plainly that everyone could understand and hear. This surely was wonderful, and the children could not make up their minds whether it was a man with goat's horns, for his long horns stuck out through two holes on either side of his cap, or a goat with a man's voice; and when the Ring Master told the children that the professor had just dropped from the sign of the Zodiac called Capricorn, which is represented in all the almanacs by a goat, they thought he must be telling the truth He did not tell them that hidden under the platform was a man that did the talking, and when the leaves of the book turned, that he was pulling a string which made them turn over, but everyone thought the goat was doing it himself.

After the performance was over, all the children as they passed fed Billy peanuts, candy, pop-corn and apples as he stood by the elephant.

Billy had behaved like a lamb for days and gone through all his performances without a hitch,— in fact he had become the pet of the circus, and allowed to roam about at will and was never tied not even at night. So this night after all had settled down and gone to bed, Billy, feeling wakeful, thought he would move around a little and take a peep into the other tents. First he stuck his nose into a little tent where they sold pop-corn, peanuts, lemonade etc., during the performances.

"Now is my chance," thought Billy, " to eat all the pop-corn I want, for I never have gotten enough to satisfy me at any one time, but how can I get it out of that glass case. It looks so easy to get at and smells so good, I must have some, even if I have to break the glass to get at it."

He stood licking the glass for a little while; then his greed getting the better of him, he backed off and gave the glass a quick hard knock with his horns. It broke and flew in all directions and let the pop-corn roll out in a perfect stream. Billy stopped to listen a minute to see if the noise of the breaking glass had brought anyone to see what was the matter, and when no one came, he commenced to eat the salted and buttered corn, and he ate until for once in his life he could say he had had enough. But, oh my! what a thirst it had given him, and he did not know where to get a drink unless he went and stole it out of the elephant's tub of water, but he did not like to go there as the elephant's keeper slept near his charge and he might catch him and tie him up.

Billy was just leaving the tent when he ran into a large tin water cooler. It took but a minute to push the top off with his nose and then he began to drink. But what was the matter with the water? It had turned sour and had round pieces of yellow, sour stuff floating in it; it was his first taste of lemonade, consequently he did not know what he was drinking.

In his disgust at finding no water, he revenged himself by upsetting the water cooler and spilling all the lemonade. Then he walked out and going into the first tent he came to, he found himself in the room of the leading lady who was fast asleep on a cot. At the end of the tent he saw a small table with a looking-glass hanging above it, but when Billy saw his reflection in it, he did not make the mistake of thinking it was another goat like he had once before. He walked up to the table and seeing a stick of red stuff that looked like candy, he ate it, but it turned out to be a stick of red paint that the leading lady used to paint her lips. After tasting her powder, and upsetting her bottle of perfumery, and chewing her blonde wig, thinking it some kind of yellow grass, he walked out without awakening her.

Next he went into a tent that had pictures of snakes of all kinds painted on it. This was the tent occupied by the snake charmers, but Billy knew nothing about large snakes, only little inoffensive garter snakes, so he went in and commenced nosing around in the baskets he saw setting there with blankets in them to see what was under the blankets.

In the first one, he felt something cold and slippery and not to his taste, so he let it alone, thinking it a piece of garden hose; but when he stuck his nose in the next basket something long and slim and pliable stuck its head out and wound itself around his body drawing itself tighter and tighter, until Billy found himself staggering for want of breath. When he was nearly squeezed to death he made a death-like groan which awoke the Indian snake charmer who was asleep in one corner of the tent on a pile of rugs. The man took in the situation at a glance, and came to Billy's rescue, making the snake uncoil itself by playing on a kind of bagpipe, a queer, weird, monotonous piece of music. This charmed the snake and it uncoiled itself from Billy and, swaying its body, crawled toward the snake charmer.

The second that Billy felt its coils slip from his body, he took a long breath and ran from the tent not even stopping to wiggle his head in thanks for his preservation. Once outside, he made his way back to his own tent where he lay down on his pile of straw to snatch a little sleep before daylight, as unconcerned as if nothing had happened.

Billy and the Snakes

THE NEXT day after Billy's midnight prowl which was Saturday, there was great commotion among the circus people, for the leading lady accused her rival, the brunette, of coming into her dressing room while she slept and destroying her blonde wig; while the pop-corn man said thieves had been at his stand and broken his glass case and eaten his pop-corn, beside they had spilled all his lemonade that he had intended using the next day; the night watchman was going to be discharged for not attending to his business; then the Indian snake charmer came along and told them the thief had visited his tent but his snakes had frightened him away.

"And he was a big fellow I can tell you. I did not dare tackle him."

"Oh my!" said the leading lady, "and to think he was in my tent and I slept through it all."

"There, I told you I did not touch your old straw colored wig!" said the brunette.

And they all said, "Do tell us all about it, what time of the night did he come, and which way did he go when he ran away?"

"All right," said the snake charmer, with a twinkle in his eye the others did not see, "sit down and I will tell you all about it,—how I was awakened by a groan, and saw standing in the middle of my tent, a huge fellow, with a long, white beard and white, agonized face; for you must know that my boa-constrictor was squeezing him to death."

"Oh, how awful! Weren't you frightened?" said the leading-lady.

"No, because I knew he could not touch me while the snake was coiled around him. At first I thought I would let the boa kill him, but he looked so awful with his eyes sticking out of his head, as the snake squeezed him tighter and tighter, that I felt sorry for him; so I began to play the music I always play when I want the snakes to come to me, and the boa stopped squeezing the goat and came to me."

"Goat, did you say? You mean burglar."

"No, I mean goat, or *burglar* if you would rather call him so, for your thief was nothing more or less than Billy Whiskers."

"You mean, horrid man to fool us so!" they all said.

And the snake charmer got up and hurried out of the tent for he saw blood in the eye of the champion boxer and he thought he had better get out before the man took hold of him.

Saturday was to be the last day of the circus in Smithville and immediately after the evening performance they were to break camp and move in the night, and be on the road all day Sunday traveling to the next town, where they were booked to give a performance on Monday morning.

Now all this meant quick work and rapid travel, as they could not go by train, there being no railroad to this town, so they had to have their circus horses and wagons move them.

When Billy heard them talking about moving, he thought it would be great fun and looked forward to it with pleasure. But he little knew what was before him.

During the morning performance Billy behaved all right, but in the afternoon he was so excited and anxious to be off that he behaved very badly. He ran around the ring so fast that when the monkey jumped through the paper hoops expecting to land on Billy's back, he was beyond him and the monkey landed on the ground and had to run to catch up. This made the ring-master angry and he hit Billy a sharp cut with his whip, but instead of making him behave better he got worse and worse. He would stand still and shake himself until he nearly made the monkey's bones crack; and when the ring-master hit him, he stood on his hind legs and the monkey had to cling to his horns to keep from falling off. When Billy found he could not throw the monkey, he ran for the pole in the center of the ring that supported the tent, and tried to butt him off but the monkey was too quick for him and dodged every time. At last Billy tried rolling with him, but this the ring-master could not allow as it would ruin the saddle strapped to his back. He gave him a few good cuts with the whip that stung like everything and this turned Billy's wrath from the monkey to him, and like a shot he was up and after the ring-master. He planted his horns in the middle of the ring-master's back and ran him to the edge of the ring where he gave him a butt that sent him flying to the other tent.

Billy was punished for this and told he should have no supper, and he understood what they said although they did not suppose he did.

"All right," he thought, "no supper, no performance, for I won't behave and take my part unless I am fed. But I will find something to eat even if they won't feed me, for a goat can eat almost anything from tin cans to apples."

The man who had tied Billy had scarcely gotten out of sight when he commenced to chew his rope in two and when it dropped apart, Billy walked over and commenced to eat the elephant's food. This the elephant did not like. He told Billy to stop and go eat his own supper, but Billy would not, neither  would he take the trouble to explain to the elephant that he hadn't any supper and was expected to go supperless. Now if he had only told the elephant, who had always

105

been a good friend of his, he would gladly have given him half of his supper; but Billy was in a contrary mood and would say nothing, but kept on eating. This provoked the elephant, so he quietly wound his trunk around Mr. Billy and lifting him from the ground, set him on top of the lion's cage that was standing near. Billy was more surprised when he found himself standing on top of the lion's cage than he had ever been in his life, but only for a minute for he jumped down and disappeared through a tear in the canvas of the tent. As he ran away he heard all the animals laughing, though you might have called it the lion's roar and the hyena's call, and above all the racket he heard the head animal keeper asking what all this racket was about; and although they all tried to tell him by each giving his particular call, he was too stupid to understand animal talk, so lost all the fun of the joke.

When Billy came through the side of the tent, he found himself near the tent where the horses and ponies were kept. Smelling corn and oats, he walked in, and while talking to his particular friends, the Shetland ponies, he helped himself to their supper.

While in this tent he became acquainted with a little Mexican Burroetta that was destined to become his closest companion and friend in the future. The Burroetta was just his height, of a mouse color, with a white streak down its spine and four white stockinged feet, but the most peculiar thing about its looks was its exceedingly long ears,—ears that were as long as Billy's horns. It was the cutest, smartest little creature you ever saw, and had most beautiful, large, liquid eyes. It looked as mild as a dove, but was quite deceiving for it was as full of the "old scratch" as Billy himself. It must have been this kindred spirit that drew them together from the first.

That night the people had come to the circus; looked at the animals and passed into the performing tent; several of the things on the programme had been gone through with and it was Billy's turn to perform next and still Billy had not been found.

Every man and woman on the place had been looking for him, but though they had hunted everywhere and inquired of every one if he had seen a large, white goat with long whiskers, no one had seen him and they were about to substitute something else for his performance when one of the men, coming into the ponies' tent for something, saw Billy lying down by the little Burroetta.

"Here Billy, you rascal, come along with me. We have been looking everywhere for you."

And Billy was led off and made to go through his performance. But to-night he was cross and still angry with the ring-master. So when about through with his imitation of the professor, he leaned over and took a mouthful of the leaves of the book and chewed them up. Then he stood up in his chair with his gown and spectacles on, and before anyone could stop him he had jumped down and ran out of the tent, with the spectacles still on his nose and his gown trailing after him.

The excitement and confusion this caused in the circus knew no bounds. And when the children discovered that the astrologer was nothing more or less than an ordinary goat, and that his voice had come from a man, who was a ventriloquist, hid under the platform, their disgust was complete and it broke up the circus performance for that night.

Billy chewed, wriggled and pulled at his gown until he tore it off and then he kicked up his heels and disappeared in the darkness outside; and he was careful to keep in the shadows away from the light, so no one could see him, for he had sense enough to know that he had done wrong and would be punished if caught.

What Billy Did === *on Sunday* ===

BILLY, after running out of the circus, stood in the shadow of a shed under a large tree. From his hiding place he could perceive all that was going on at the circus as it was bright moonlight, beside all the workmen had lights fastened in their caps so they could see without the bother of carrying a lantern around.

First Billy saw them hitch the draft-horses to the animal wagons and vehicles they had for carrying baggage. Then the big tent closed as if it were an umbrella, and it was rolled up and put in a wagon made purposely for hauling it; then all the riding horses with the men and women performers on their backs, started the procession. Next came the cages filled with animals and last the baggage vans and feed wagons.

After they were well on their way Billy trotted on behind keeping well in the shadows. They had been crawling silently along the highways like a huge snake for a long while when all of a sudden the long line came to a sudden halt.

There was great noise and confusion ahead and, of course, Billy's curiosity called him to the front immediately to see what was the matter. In passing the wagons which had been left by their drivers to go forward and find out the cause of the sudden stop, Billy accidently ran into his friend, Senorita Burroetta, which means Miss Baby Buro, as his friend was called.

"How are you, Betty?" For in their short acquaintance Billy had shortened her name to that. "I did not know you with that pack on your back. Aren't you tired carrying that heavy load?"

"Yes," answered Betty, "and the girth pinches me. They did not get it on straight and every time I step it hurts me awfully."

"Here let me see if I can't fix it," said Billy.

"Oh never mind, I can stand it, for it isn't the first time they have buckled a piece of skin in; beside you could not unbuckle it with your teeth .or feet."

"No, but I can chew the girth in two if you don't mind being pinched a little more while I am doing it," said Billy.

So Billy commenced to chew the girth which he could get at easily where it stuck out from Betty's side to pass over the load on her back; and we know better than Betty that Billy was good at chewing rope and straps in two. Soon the girth began to give and Betty swelled herself out and the girth split in two and let the load on her back slip to the ground.

Then the goat and Burro ran ahead to see what all the scolding and loud talking were about. When they got there, they found the elephant had broken down a little bridge that crossed the narrow stream and there was no way to get the wagons over. The elephant, before crossing, had put his forefoot out to try the strength of the bridge and with a little shake the bridge had collapsed and dropped into the water. Had he stepped on it without trying it, he would most likely have been killed for it surely would have gone down with him on it.

The only way now to get across was for the wagons to drive down the steep embankment, through the water and up the other side. This they proceeded to do, but Billy and Betty jumped the space. Then they scampered on ahead after the horseback riders who had gone before.

As they ran they could hear the lion's roar and the hyena's laugh when their cages were driven into the water, and the water rose on them, while the elephants kept up such a trumpeting that it awoke all the country folks who were near enough to hear it, and they thought the Day of Judgment had come and it was Gabriel's trumpet they heard.

A poor, ignorant Swedish family that lived on the bank of the stream by the bridge were awakened by the noise but were afraid to get up and look out of the window to see what all the commotion was about.

At last the brave husband by coaxing and threatening succeeded in getting his wife out of bed. As she had never been to a circus in her life or seen anything but the picture of wild animals, she was nearly frightened to death at what she saw passing in the moonlight, and ran back to bed and put her head under the covers and would not speak a word, though her husband threatened to kick her out of bed. Poor woman, she could not tell him what she saw, for she did not know the name of the animals.

At last her husband got up courage enough to go to the window and look out as his wife had, but he stayed less time than she did for just as he got there the lions gave a mighty roar and all the animals followed suit, for the lions' cage was passing through the water and they did not like the cold water crawling up their legs and of course they thought they were going to be drowned; while the Swedish workman thought he was going to be chewed up alive, and flew back to bed with teeth chattering and held on to his wife for protection; and had a lion really come after them he would probably have thrown his wife at the lion's head for him to eat, while he made good his escape.

All this time Billy and Betty were trotting along side by side gossiping about people in the circus, and all the time it became lighter and lighter as it was getting nearer sunrise.

About five o'clock they saw, away in the blue distance, a tall church steeple and they knew they must be nearing the town where the circus was to be held.

As they came nearer they could hear the sound of the church bell ring out on the stillness, calling the people to early morning mass, and soon they could see the people going to church, and the mothers take their children by the hand and pull them into the church as they did not want them to see anything so wicked as a circus procession on Sunday morning.

Billy noticing this, said, "Let us give the children a treat. When the people are all in the church we will walk in and see what it looks like inside."

The two mischief-makers hung around out of sight, until the people had stopped going in, then they walked boldly into the vestibule. Here they saw a marble basin filled with clear, cool-looking water. They stopped and drank it, not knowing it was the holy water the Catholics cross themselves with before entering church.

The church aisle was separated from the vestibule only by two green baize doors. These Billy and Betty pushed open with their noses and while the organ was playing and the priests were kneeling, Billy and Betty walked the whole length of the middle aisle, side by side, as if they were a bridal couple. When they arrived at the altar, Billy stopped and commenced to eat some roses that were in a vase on the altar steps.

The congregation sat stupefied with horror to see these animals in church and directly behind the kneeling priest and choir boys. The music made Betty lonesome and she threw up her head and let out such a loud, mule-like bray that it frightened the kneeling priest and he jumped up as if shot for he thought he had heard Balaam's ass bray; but when he turned and saw standing behind him a live burro and a goat, his astonishment knew no bounds and he stood gazing at them with open mouth, while the choir boys laughed and giggled and thought it a good joke.

Soon the ushers and deacons came to their senses enough to come forward and try to drive the beasts out. But when Billy

114

saw them coming he ran up the altar steps into the pulpit, and Betty ran through the first door she saw open, which proved not to be the outer door but one which led into the room where the choir boys dressed.

When Betty appeared there, the boys laughed and screamed and drove her out into the church again, and kicking up her heels she ran out of the church, braying for Billy. When Billy saw her go he ran down the altar steps, upsetting a near-sighted deacon who was coming up to help drive him out, and bleating to Betty that he was coming he rushed through the door.

They trotted along side by side down the street until they came to a beautiful place surrounded by a tall, iron fence. Through the fence they could see a large, brick residence with a cupola on top. On one side of the house was the flower garden, while on the other a fruit patch and vegetable garden. And oh, how good the fresh, green lettuce and beet tops looked to these tired, hungry travelers.

"Let us go in and help ourselves," said Billy.

"We can't get through the fence," said Betty, "and it is too high to jump."

"You remind me of Nanny, for she was always finding objections and obstacles to everything I wanted to do."

"Well, who in the world is Nanny? I should like to know," said Betty.

"Why haven't I told you about her?" asked Billy.

"No, you have not, Billy Whiskers, and I should like to know right away."

"Well, I will tell you, Senorita Borroetta, and you need not be so cross about it either. She is my wife and a sweeter, dearer little wife no goat ever had before!"

Betty stopped stock still in the road and glared at Billy for a second, before she could speak from astonishment. Then she said: "Billy Whiskers you are a gay deceiver and you know you never told me you were married and I am sure I always thought you were a bachelor."

"I am very sorry if it makes any difference to you, but I never told you because we have been so busy talking of other things and I have not had a chance."

"Oh, very well then," said Betty, "I will forgive you if you did not mean to keep it from me."

So the two made up and commenced to look for a gate or way to get into the garden. At last they saw where an iron bar or two of the fence had been broken, making quite a good-sized hole and through this they squeezed themselves and were soon having a feast off of Deacon Jones's prize cabbages, lettuce and beets, while the family, including the Deacon, were at church.

They were still eating when they heard the iron gates shut with a clang and looking up they saw the Deacon coming toward them, swinging his cane in frantic anger, showing that he had already forgotten his Sunday-school lesson: "Let not your angry passions rise."

Billy, with a mouthful of carrots, started to run toward the stables, trusting to find a way out and Betty with a twist of her body and a squeal followed after him.

They were just going into the barn, the door of which was standing open, when a little, yellow dog ran out at them and commenced to bark and bite at Betty's heels. She let one foot fly out quickly behind and Mr. Doggie went rolling over in the dirt, and at that minute Billy spied a little open

117

gate that led into the orchard and through this they both ran with the Deacon and dog still after them.

When they got to the other side of the orchard they came to a rail fence. This Billy took at one jump, breaking the top rail as he went over, and it was a good thing he did for it helped Betty get over as she was not as high a jumper as Billy.

They were over the fence and a good way down the road before the deacon got to the fence, and then he was so out of breath from running that he gave up the chase, called off his dog, and throwing two or three stones at them, turned and walked slowly back to the garden to see what damage they had done.

Billy and Betty wandered around all day and at night went to sleep in a straw stack on the outskirts of the town.

What Billy Did on Monday

ALL DAY Sunday the circus people worked to get their tents up and everything in shape for the Monday's performances, and when at night they went to look over the animals to see if all were there they missed Billy and Betty.

"Now there will be the dickens to pay," said the animal keeper, "if that goat can't be found for he has been the means of bringing more children to the circus than anything else we have had for them."

"I will eat my shirt off if I know where to look for him! You can bet your life he is a good one on a hide."

"You and I will have to go hunt him, John, so go saddle two horses and we will start out. He must have turned into some of the lanes we passed on our way here, and coaxed

Betty off with him. They could easily get away without being noticed when the bridge broke down. You search the town and I will take the road and lanes."

While the men were looking for the two runaways, they were quietly grazing along the road that led to the town.

Now Billy got tired of the quiet and said, "Come Betty, let's go into the town and see the sights and have some fun, and maybe we can find a grocery store where there are good things setting outside to eat, or a fruit stand," for Billy had not forgotten how luscious the pears and peaches had tasted that he had stolen from a fruit stand one day.

This was agreeable to Betty and the two trotted along side by side toward the town. Presently they came to a large sign-board on which pictures of the circus were posted. There Billy spied himself pictured as trotting along with the monkey riding on his back and jumping through the paper hoops.

At sight of the monkey Billy got mad, as usual, and before Betty knew what he was going to do, he ran up to the fence and commenced trying to butt it down, calling to Betty to come help kick it over.

They were thus employed when a farmer came along the road and, seeing them, took out his whip and drove them off.

120

WHAT BILLY DID ON MONDAY

They ran along before him for a while and then dropped back until he had passed them. As soon as he had passed, Billy spied on the back of his wagon a large basket of celery with the tops sticking out over the edge.

"Look, Betty, look!" cried Billy, pointing his nose in the direction of the wagon. "Let's follow on behind and eat up his celery. It will be a good joke on him." And the two scampered after the farmer and soon caught up, for he was driving slowly; and he could not see them for the things that were piled up high behind him.

When the two rascals caught up to the wagon they ate all the celery they wanted, which was more than half of it, as it was deliciously juicy and tasted fine. They had had no breakfast except some dusty grass that grew beside the road.

While they ate the farmer whistled low to himself and planned how he would sell his celery to the grocery man; and then, with the money, go to the circus, and see the wonderful astrologer that was neither goat nor man who was advertised to perform. He little guessed that the "Wonderful Astrologer" was at that moment eating up his celery and making it doubtful whether he would have any left or not.

Billy and Betty were still eating when a dog spied them and ran out from his yard after them. Billy turned and tried to hook him but the dog was too quick. He dodged, but in trying to escape from Billy he got too near Betty's heels and she gave him a kick in the side that sent him rolling over into the dust, yelping, and before he could get up Billy helped him up by sticking his horns under him and tossing him over the fence.

The owner of the dog saw this and ran out calling for the farmer to stop or he would have him arrested for allowing his goat to hook his dog. The farmer stopped to see what all the row was about, and while the owner of the dog was shaking his fist in the farmer's face, and the farmer was trying to explain that the goat and mule, as he called Betty, did not belong to him, Billy and Betty sneaked off and disappeared down a side road and to their surprise found themselves facing the circus tents.

If they went forward the circus people would catch them, and if they went back, the angry man and farmer would be after them. As they stood discussing which way to go, it was decided for them, for the animal keeper on his horse turned into the lane behind them and drove them to the circus in double-quick time with his long whip.

All the way there he scolded them as he tried to crack them with his whip, and it was no fun being hit with it as it seemed to take a piece of flesh out each   time it struck.

Betty ran in among the Shet-land ponies where she belonged and Billy dodged into the first tent he saw with the flap open. For a wonder it turned out to be the one where he  belonged, and in less time than it takes to tell it Billy found himself chained beside the elephant.

"There, Master Billy, I guess you won't chew yourself loose in a hurry again, and have me chasing all over the country for you," said the animal keeper.

And to make up for his past bad behavior Billy performed better the next day than he had at any time.

What Billy Did on Tuesday

TUESDAY turned out to be a dismal, cold, rainy day and Billy was glad enough to stay quietly in the tent. He thought it would be a good chance to become better acquainted with the animals in the cages and he decided to call on them all by beginning at one cage and visiting each in order until he had completed the circle.

He could not stay where he was, for Nancy, the old maid camel, made him nervous; she talked so much, and when she was not talking she chewed her cud like an old maid chews gum.

"How can you stand her?" Billy whispered to the elephant.

"Oh, I have got used to it," said the elephant, "and I don't hear her half the time, and when she gets *too* bad I just pull the flops of my ears down tight to my head, and I can't hear a word. And then I set my trunk to wobbling and make it nod 'yes' half the time and 'no' the other, and I find it answers quite well."

"But how do you know when to say 'yes' and when to say 'no'?" Billy asked.

"I don't mind if I do answer wrong part of the time, and if I get too much off she stops talking altogether and that pleases me better, so you see it answers very well."

"But don't you get tired leading such an inactive life?" asked Billy.

"I used to," answered the elephant, "when I was younger, and before my mate died. But since she died and I have rheumatism I don't seem to care much, for without her there would be nothing to do if I did run away; beside your climate is so cold, and your forests so skinny and bare looking there would not be any fun living in them."

"Our forests skinny and bare looking, did you say? You don't know what you are talking about. I guess our forests are as nice as yours in India, and not half so full of snakes and chattering monkeys, to say nothing of the nasty crocodiles and hippopotamuses that you have in your rivers; and vines growing all over the trees and from one tree to another, so thickly you can't walk without making a path for yourself by breaking them down."

"Oh, but that is just what I like," said the elephant, "and the air is so hot and moist you feel fine, while here you are either all dried up with heat or shivering with cold."

"Well, every one to his taste, I suppose," and he walked over to the hyenas' cage to make their acquaintance, out of curiosity, as he knew little about hyenas.

"My, aren't they homely, sneaky, shifty-eyed looking things!" thought Billy. "I would not like to meet one alone after dark, but still I hear they are cowardly and wait until one is dead before they try to eat him up. I don't think I will make a long call, for they grin and laugh too much, and their laughter has no mirth in it. It is just a loud guffaw." So he only stayed a few minutes and then went on to a beautiful white llama's cage.

"Good morning, Miss Llama," said Billy very politely, for he wished to get in the good graces of the beautiful Miss Llama whom he admired very much for her long, silky, white hair and mild, brown eyes.

"Good morning, Mr. Whiskers," she replied. "How do you find yourself after our Saturday night's trip?"

"Very well," said Billy, "but I am afraid you must have had a bad shaking up where the bridge was broken, if you had to go down that steep embankment to cross the creek."

"You are right; it was steep," said the llama, "and I was nearly scared to death when I felt the water running into my cage and I had just given myself up as lost when it commenced to recede, and I was thrown on my knees by the cage being pulled with a jerk up the opposite bank. How did you get across?"

"Oh, easily! I just jumped across from one pier of the bridge to the other," said Billy. "I met a friend of mine and we went off and had a fine time. How I wish you could get out of that cage, so you could go with us sometime!"

"You don't wish it more than I do, and it always makes me weep, when we are driven along the sweet smelling roads, to think that I can't get out and must be shut in here for life."

"It really is a shame, for you are too pretty to be shut in a cage. Are you sure you can't break some of those bars some night and get out?"

"I am sure," said the llama, "for I have tried time and again."

"Well, Billy Whiskers, you are the 'consarnedest' goat I ever knew, and how in the 'dickens' you managed to break that chain is more than I can tell," Billy and Miss Llama heard someone say behind them and looking round they saw the animal keeper.

"So, so; you simply pulled up the stake you were tied to when you found you could not chew your chain in two, did you? Well, come along with me; you have been idle long enough, and we are going to teach you some new tricks."

When Billy heard this his heart sank for he disliked the ring-master and was afraid they would make him stand on his hind-legs and walk. Had he only known it, that was the easiest thing he would have to do. He was led to the performing ring and there stood the hated ring-master facing a line of animals standing in a straight line reaching from one side of the ring to the other. In the middle stood the elephant, with the summer house, as Billy called it, on his back; next him stood a camel; next the camel a giraffe; next the giraffe a horse; next the horse, a zebra, and last a little Shetland pony. On the other side of the elephant were more animals standing in the same order.

"What in the world can they want of me," thought Billy, but he soon found out for they dressed him up as a clown in a white suit with red spots on it and tied a mask on his face and a pointed clown's cap on his head. Then they led him to where the pony stood and made him walk up a step ladder, onto a little platform, strapped to the pony's back. From this he was made to walk up another step onto a similar platform on the zebra's back; here he was made to stop and make a bow and so on until he had reached the little summer house on the elephant's back. This he was made to enter and sit upright on a little seat that was inside while the elephant started forward and walked out of the ring carrying Billy with him.

After this he was dressed as a workman, with a pipe in his mouth and a hod of mortar strapped to his shoulder, and made to walk part way round the ring on his hind legs. Then he was allowed to rest and was given a bunch of

129

carrots to eat. While he was eating these Betty was brought in hitched to a little low wheeled cart. Then a great Dane dog was brought in hitched to a similar cart. After that a man pulled in another cart like the other two and hitched Billy to that. The carts were painted red, white, and blue and trimmed with flags. Soon three little dogs dressed as ladies were carried in, put into the carts with the reins over their necks. Then the goat, burro, and dog were put neck to neck, ready to start on the race that was to begin when the ring-master cracked his whip.

At the signal the dog got started ahead, but half way around the ring Billy passed him; the next time around, the dog was again ahead, when slow little Betty balked in the middle of the course and both the goat and dog ran into her upsetting the carts and spilling out the little lady dog drivers. None of them were hurt and the little dogs ran around stepping on their silk petticoats and getting their hats askew, they enjoying the upset by barking and making all the noise they could.

"Well, boys, you want to do it better at the regular performance," said the ring-master, as the animals were led from the ring.

What Billy Did on Wednesday

WEDNESDAY, Billy was not tied up and after wandering around the circus and visiting the different animals and stopping to chat with Betty, he decided to watch his chance and slip into town.

This was not hard for him to do and he soon found himself on the main street. At first he walked quietly along looking into the windows, but presently he saw before him a well-known figure, that of the ring-master.

"Now is my chance," thought Billy, "to get even with him for giving me all those cuts with his whip. I'll just give him a butt and land him in the middle of that mud puddle, and I am going to do it so hard he will hear his spine crack and I guess he won't hit me with his whip again very soon."

So Billy started quietly on a run, going on his tiptoes so the ring-master would not hear him until it was too late to get out of the way. Just as Billy got to him the man raised his arm to doff his hat to a pretty girl, and the next thing he knew he was flying through the air with his hat in his hand. Still holding his arm extended, he landed in the deep puddle of muddy water in the middle of the street, while the young lady threw up her hands and fled.

It is needless to say that Billy immediately disappeared down a side street. Here he ran into a livery stable where a dog fight had been going on in the back yard. Two ferocious bull-dogs, had fought so wickedly that their jaws had had to be pried apart.

One of the dogs had a chain around its neck and its owner was going to lead it off when one of the livery men saw Billy and called out:

WHAT BILLY DID ON WEDNESDAY

"Wait a minute Mr. Pride, here's a Billy goat I bet can lick your dog. Let us turn them loose in the yard and have another fight."

"Why, man what are you talking about? My dog would make just one grab at the goat's throat and kill him."

"I am not so sure of that," replied the man, "but I am mighty sure he will lick your dog if he is the goat I think he is, for I believe he is the trained goat from the circus."

"Let's have a fight," said the other men that were standing around. "It will be great sport to see the goat lick the dog that can whip every other dog in town."

"So you think the goat can lick my dog, do you? I'll bet one or all of you twenty dollars that he can't."

"It is a go!" said two or three. Then the man that had proposed the fight said: "It is all well enough to have a little fight for fun but I hate to see your dog killed, as he may be."

"Oh, don't you worry about my dog. Leave all your worrying for the goat."

All this time the dog had been pulling at his chain and straining to get at the goat, while Billy quietly walked around inspecting things, chewing anything he could find.

"Won't I fix that conceited dog!" said Billy to himself. So he allowed himself to be driven into the back-yard. Here the men formed a circle with Billy in the center; then the man unfastened the chain from the dog's neck. With a rush he went for the goat, who quickly stood on his hind legs, lowered his head and met the dog's onslaught with his horns, running one of them into his chest, which sent the blood spitting out. Then the dog tried to get behind Billy for another charge but Billy wheeled and met him again as before and no matter which way the dog tried to approach him, Billy was always head foremost with his long, pointed horns sticking straight out to meet him.

The dog was getting more and more furious at each failure and at last he made a blind plunge at the goat, but, as before, Billy was too quick for him and this time he sent the dog yelping back to his master.

"Here! what do you mean by shutting our goat up?" they heard someone say and turning around they saw one of the men from the circus who had been sent out to look for Billy as it was nearly time for the performance to begin.

"We did not shut him up. He walked in of his own accord; but you should have been here a minute sooner and you would have seen the prettiest fight you ever saw in your life, between your goat and the bulliest bull-dog of the town."

"I am sorry I did not see it; but perhaps we can have another sometime."

"Never!" said the dog's owner very emphatically. "I doubt if he lives through this."

"Well, good-bye, boys; come and see Billy Whiskers perform in the circus this afternoon and you will see as good a performance as fighting, and I'll give all passes who bet on him this time.

"Billy, I would not have given much for your skin after the ring-master got through with you if it had not been for this fight; but now I think he will forgive you for the butt you gave him this morning, since you whipped Mr. Pride's dog for he hates Mr. Pride because he forbade him calling on his daughter."

What Billy Did on Thursday =

T

HURSDAY there was no performance as the circus was to break camp and move to the next town where they were to take the train for a large city. Here they would meet the rest of the circus which had been divided up into small bands and sent into the country, like the one Billy was now with. When they met in the city, all the companies joined forces.

The elephant told Billy to wait and see what elegant performances they gave when they were all together. "Why!" he said, "we have three rings with acting going on in each one at the same time, and all the performers wear their best clothes and try their best to outshine each other; beside we have three or four times as many animal side-tents as we do now.

WHAT BILLY DID ON THURSDAY

"When we meet I will introduce you to my chum who is the oldest and largest elephant in the circus business. He is a fine fellow and tells a good story, and one could listen for hours to him telling of his adventures and experiences while in the jungle and traveling in this country. But it nearly makes him weep when he tells of how he was once the pet elephant of a Prince of India and how the Prince would never ride any other but himself when hunting or riding in the royal processions. 'Only think of the come-down,' he used to add, 'from having a Prince of the royal blood on your back to a common circus rider in gaudy skirts! Then my blankets and trappings were of velvet, studded with real precious stones. Now they are velveteen with glass to imitate the precious jewels. Oh, dear! Oh, dear! That I should ever live to see this day.'"

Here the elephant's conversation was cut short by someone screaming, "Fire, fire!"

"Where? where?" called Billy who was all excitement in a minute and he started to run in the direction he heard the voice come from, but alas for Billy! He forgot he was tied until he came to the end of his rope and it gave him a quick jerk which sent him head over heels, breaking the rope.

"Gee whiz! I nearly broke my neck. Blame their old rope!"

"Fire, fire, fire!" called the voice again, followed by a laugh and Billy, looking up, saw a green poll-parrot swinging on a

rope overhead, that commenced to call: "April fool, April fool!" as loud as she could.

"How I do hate parrots and monkeys! I dare you to come down here, you disagreeable, impertinent, pea-green, old maid of a bird!" bleated Billy.

WHAT BILLY DID ON THURSDAY

He had hardly gotten the words out of his mouth when something struck him on the back and began to pull his hair out by the roots. It was Miss Polly who had dropped like a torpedo and who was screeching, pecking and clawing him at a great rate. She was in a bad humor that day as they had forgotten to feed her her accustomed crackers and coffee.

As soon as Billy got over his surprise, which was in a second, he lay down and rolled. This knocked Polly off but the minute he stopped she flew onto his back again and pecked him until the blood ran. The second time she lit on his back he thought of a way to get even. He saw the elephant's tub of water a little way before him and with two bounds he was by its side and before Miss Polly was aware of what was up, she found herself doused in the tub, and when she came up from under the water there was no goat in sight.

As Billy went out of the tent he ran into the animal keeper who was just coming in.

"Ho, ho! Master Billy, not so fast. I was coming to look for you, for we are about to start and you have a way of turning up missing just when you are most wanted." As he said this he caught hold of the piece of rope around Billy's neck that Billy had broken when he took his somersault, and said: "Come along with me. I am going to put you for once where you can't get out, no matter how hard you bite, chew or kick."

"I wonder what he is going to do with me," thought Billy.

But he soon found out, for the man led him to a vacant cage that a wild cat had died in the day before, and made him walk up an inclined board into it.

"Heavens!" thought Billy, "I'll never get out of here unless I die and am carried out like the wild cat was, and if I don't die I know I will go crazy, shut up in a little cooped up place like this, with only room enough to take one step and not enough to turn around unless you turn yourself in sections."

"Well, Billy, how do you like being caged?" asked the animal keeper.

"Yes, you vicious beast, you, how do you like being shut up where you can't butt and send people flying into mud-puddles and chew up their wigs, etc.?" asked the ring-master who had joined the animal keeper.

"Oh, it is you, is it? Well, you just wait until I get out of here and see where I will butt you next time, and the animal

140

keeper, too," bleated Billy, but neither of them understood what he said.

When they left him alone Billy tried every way he could think of to break out, but he could make no impression on the iron bars, chew as he would,—in fact, he broke one of his teeth trying. Then he tried butting out the ends of the cage, but it was of no use. Next he stood on his hind legs and tried to push the roof off with his long horns, but to no effect; so he lay down tired and broken-hearted on the hard bottom of the cage and gave himself up to the blues.

He was lying there quietly, apparently asleep, when a man brought him a bundle of hay to eat, a bucket of water to drink and a pitch-fork of straw to lie on.

Billy did not move when they brought the things, pretending to be asleep, but he was rudely awakened out of his supposed sleep by the man sticking the prongs of the pitchfork into him to make him get up so he could spread the straw on the bottom of the cage. He felt too disheartened to eat, especially food which he detested, but thought he would take a drink as he was very thirsty, but at one smell of the bucket he turned up his aristocratic nose for he detected the bucket had not been washed since it had been used by some of the other animals for he could smell and see their hairs on the rim; so he lay down more disgusted than ever. Poor Billy's confinement was going to be hard for him. He had roamed the fields and towns, master of himself, too long to take to being shut up easily.

At last Billy fell asleep and only awakened when they hitched the horses to the wagon-like cage he was in to draw it to the depot. Just before they started he heard a man say: "Here, you forgot to put up the sides on that cage with the goat in."

Then the man brought wooden sides and fastened them onto the cage over the iron bars. This left Billy only a little iron barred opening near the top, at one side, to get air through.

"I shall surely smother," thought Billy. "Oh, this is horrible! I feel as if I were buried alive."

At that minute the horses started up and poor Billy went down on his knees with a sudden jerk.

"How I wish Nanny was here to comfort me," thought Billy. "She was always so patient and cheerful." How like a man that was for Billy to forget all about Nanny while he was free and having a good time, but the minute he was in trouble to think of her and be willing to have her shut up if he could only see her.

WHAT BILLY DID ON THURSDAY

After several hours of hard traveling they stopped, and Billy knew they must be at the depot for he heard the engines whistling and the bells ringing, and he was very glad of it for his knees were all skinned from slipping on the floor from one end of the cage to the other when they went up or down hill, for it was impossible to stand, so he had to lay down and make the best of it.

"I never pitied caged animals before," thought Billy, "but I did not know what they had to endure or I should."

After a great deal of commotion, swearing and fussing on the part of the men outside, Billy's cage was at last on board and the train started.

"Mercy!" thought Billy, "aren't they going to give me a drink of water or something fresh and cool to eat? Do they expect me to eat that dried up, tasteless, weedy hay this hot day; and as for the water, that got upset the first hill we went up. Oh, dear! and to add to the rest of my troubles I have got a cinder in my eye, along with this horrible dust that is blowing in that stuffy little window and I know I am going to be smothered to death. Oh, if Nanny were only here, to lick this cinder out of my eye! It smarts so I wish I had hands instead of feet for once in my life so I could get it out. I

143

wonder if people ever think how inconvenient it is not to have hands sometimes."

And poor old Billy commenced to cry softly to himself. It was a good thing he did for he soon cried the cinder out and when his eye stopped hurting, he got some of his spunk back again and began to plan some way of getting out of his cage.

At twelve o'clock at night they reached the city and were driven through the silent streets to a vacant lot where all the circus bands were to meet. And here I will leave Billy until next morning.

What Billy Did on Friday

 WHEN Billy's little band of circus people joined the others they found everything in order as they were the last company of the six traveling bands to join the main one.

There was one huge tent with three rings in it where the performances would be given; opening into this was another large one where the animals were exhibited and branching out of this were three others,—one where the horses and ponies were kept; another used as the dressing room, and still another where the circus people took their meals, while scattered around were ten or a dozen sideshows.

The cage Billy was in had hardly been put in place when the sides were taken off and he found himself in the large animal tent with the cages arranged round the edge and his old

145

friend the elephant tethered just outside with the other elephants from the different bands, and his elephant friend was talking to his chum, the elephant he had told Billy about, that told such good stories. Billy thought he must be telling one now for they were both laughing, but you might have thought they were trumpeting had you heard them.

Billy bleated to the elephant and he raised his head and looked in all directions to see where Billy was but he could not see him, until Billy told him where to look.

"Goodness gracious me! Is that you, Mr. Billy, shut up in that cage? I never expected to see you in a place like that."

"Neither did I ever expect to find myself in one like this," Billy answered, "and what is more, I would rather be dead than stay here. But I will get out yet, don't you fear."

"I bet you do, Mr. Whiskers, for you are a good one at getting out of scrapes as well as getting into them. Let me introduce you to my friend and chum, Prince Nan-ka-poo, as he is called on the show bill."

After the introduction Billy's friend said: "Don't look so down hearted. I will get the Prince to tell us one of his funny stories so we can have a good laugh. He has just been telling me a capital one."

But before he had time to tell it a man came along with a hose and began to wash out Billy's cage and souse him with water, squirting it in his eyes just to tease him, which Billy thought was a little too much as it was like kicking a fellow when he was down and could not help himself.

"Just wait, Mr. Man with the hose, until I meet you when I get out of here, and if I don't make your body ache, then my name is not Billy Whiskers. I am going to give you a butt and hook that will send you half way up a telegraph pole!"

While he was fuming about this, another man came along and gave him a nice, cool drink, and as he saw he had not eaten any of the hay he gave him a bunch of carrots and a bundle of nice grass. This Billy appreciated and said to himself: "That's a nice man. I'll do him a favor some time if I ever get the chance."

Billy had not stopped eating when a man came along with a bucket in his hand with something black in it and a large flat brush. When he got to Billy's cage he commenced to unlock the door and to Billy's surprise he climbed in and shut the door after him.

"Well, I wonder what is up now," thought Billy.

"I don't want to interrupt your breakfast, Master Billy, but this job has to be done before the circus begins this morning.

147

Just go on eating while I turn you from an ordinary white goat into a black one. Hereafter you are to be known as the wild goat with three horns from Guinea. If you don't believe me, read the printed sign outside tacked to your cage, but do not be alarmed, this black stuff is not paint and it will wash off easily, for it is only charcoal and some other mixture. You see our black goat died and as we have it advertised, we are going to fix you up to represent it and the people won't know the difference for the public are easily fooled. And for your third horn—this came off of a Mexican steer."

The man took from his pocket a long horn and glued it on-to Billy's head between his other horns, only with the curved point forward instead of backward. How Billy wished for a mirror to see himself when the man had finished!

"I must look like Satan, Mr. Windlass's goat," thought Billy.

Billy did not get fixed any too soon for the people now began to crowd into the circus to see the animals before the performances commenced and they passed around the ring before the animals' cages, talking and giving them peanuts, pop-corn and apples. He heard some one say when in front of his cage:

WHAT BILLY DID ON FRIDAY

"Oh, my! Look at this queer looking goat with three horns—don't he look fierce?"

"Let's read the card on his cage and see what it says about him. It says he was caught in the mountains of Guinea and that he is very ferocious. He looks it, doesn't he? How would you like to have him hook you?" Billy heard one little boy say to another. "Isn't this funny, the card says he kills his prey with his two sharp pointed horns and then hooks the other one into his prey and carries it off."

"Is that what the card says? Well, if that isn't the biggest lie I ever heard!" thought Billy. "I'll bet the ring-master made that up, like the one about my being an astrologer. Oh, he is a dandy, he is! But when I come to think of it, I don't mind if they do fool the people, if they are so easily gulled as that; and I guess I will help them carry it out by behaving fierce and kicking around when anyone looks into my cage."

After the people had all passed into the main tent, the wind began to blow a perfect hurricane and the rain came down in sheets while one peal of thunder followed another in such quick succession that one would hardly have time to die away before another was upon it; rolling and booming like heavy pieces of artillery. The lightning was so vivid and bright that it made Billy wink at every flash.

Presently a fiercer, stronger volume of wind hit the big tent and it collapsed burying all the people under it, while the same gust swept on and picked up the tent Billy was sheltered in and carried it off, upsetting cage after cage of animals as it flew up and soared over their heads.

Billy's cage was among those upset, but before it went over the wind picked it up, carried it a few feet and then dropped it, smashing in the wooden side and setting Billy free. For once the old saying came true: "That it is an ill wind that blows nobody any good." With a swish of his stubby tail Billy was off down a side street, and as he ran he could hear above the peals of the thunder and the rushing of the wind, the lions roaring and the elephants trumpeting for fear amid the confusion and excitement of the collapsed tents,—the circus that Billy had escaped from for good.

"OH, MY! LOOK AT THIS QUEER-LOOKING GOAT WITH THREE HORNS. DON'T
HE LOOK FIERCE?"

See p. 149.

Billy Finds Nanny

As BILLY trotted down the side street, the cyclone still raged and blew loose boards and papers in every direction, but he kept on until he found himself out of the town and on the high road.

"Why, how good it seems to get away from the smelly old circus and be free again. Who cares for the wind and weather when one is free? This rain will wash the black stuff off my coat that circus fellow put on; and now I think of it, I'll just walk up to that board fence and butt off this old horn that they glued to my head: that will be the end of the Wild Goat from Guinea."

Suiting the action to the words, he walked up to the fence and hooked the curved part of the horn over the rail, pulled back, and the horn came off easily without pulling out any hair

152

as the rain had softened the glue. As it fell inside the fence, Billy kicked up his heels, whisked his stubby tail, and started down the road at a fast trot. As he ran, he made up his mind he would find Nanny once more, even if he had to spend the rest of his life looking for her. You know from past experience that if Billy made up his mind to do a thing, that he did it; for Billy's strong points were bravery, perseverance and stick-to-ativeness. These are good qualities for boys and girls to have as well as goats.

It was a good thing that Billy had these qualities, or he never would have found Nanny again. For one whole month he hunted for her, going up one road and down another, being stoned by boys and chased by men as he tried to steal a meal out of their gardens. Some times he wandered into a yard to get something to eat, and they set the dogs on him, but this they always wished they had not done, for he invariably turned and ripped the dogs open with his long horns.

In this way he traveled, sleeping by the wayside in all kinds of weather, until even he was beginning to get discouraged. When one day he happened on a road that looked familiar to him, and the further he traveled, the more familiar it became, until he came to a bridge with a red house beside it. Then he knew where he was for he recognized the house and the scenery around as the place where the bridge had broken down when the elephant had attempted to cross it. His joy knew no bounds for now all he had to do to get to Nanny was to follow this road to the town and then take another to the other side of town which would lead him to his little wife Nanny.

When he thought of dear, patient, little Nanny, a tear rolled down his cheek; but he shook it off in a hurry for the next minute the thought came to him, what if Nanny had given him up as lost and married another? The thought made him mad; and for three or four miles he ran like a steam-engine, snorting with rage as he went, and vowing to himself that if it were so, he would split her new husband open with his long horns, as he had the dogs he had met by the way.

In the meantime, while Billy had been away, poor, lonely, little Nanny had never forgotten her old Billy, though all the young Billy Goats in the herd tried to make her do so, and each and all had wanted her to marry them, but she said "no" and remained faithful to her Billy.

She had one thing to comfort her however, and that was two beautiful little Kids that had been born to her some time after the circus-man had taken Billy away. With these she spent all her time, and they repaid it by being very fond of her; and it was a beautiful sight to see the three playing together in the green meadow down by the stream.

So Billy thought the next day, when, after traveling all night, he at last came to the farm and looking through the fence saw Nanny lying in the grass with the two little kids jumping over her and kissing her nose.

"Two very fine looking kids," thought Billy. "I wonder whose they are."

Then his old heart stood still for his next thought was: "She has forgotten me, is married again and these are her children."

This thought made him feel sick and faint, and his knees shook under him, so he dropped on the grass with his nose through the rails of the fence, and there he lay for a long while, but he never took his eyes off the three in the pasture.

"I will lie here and see if it is so," thought Billy, "and if it is, I will go away and never let her know that I came back."

As he looked, old Satan, the minister that had married them, came up to speak to Nanny, and Billy felt his blood beginning to boil for he thought:

"If she is married to that old widower, and I am afraid she is, for one of those kids is as black as Satan himself, I can't stand it! I shall stay to make myself known just long enough to kill him."

Soon, however, Satan walked off, as it was getting dark, and the goats began to find cozy places for themselves for the night. But Billy lay still and watched, though he was very thirsty and hungry, not having eaten anything all day, as he had been too anxious to get back to see if Nanny was married again.

He watched her wash the kids' little faces for the night with her soft tongue and give them a good-night kiss on their little noses before they cuddled down to sleep beside her. It made Billy groan with lonesomeness to see it all, and he lay there broken in spirit and wished he could die, and closed his eyes to shut out the sight.

But he could not keep them closed. He had to open them to look once more on Nanny's sweet, patient face. As he did so, he noticed that the moon was just rising; and as it came up, Nanny rose also and stepping carefully so as not to waken her babies, she walked toward the fence where Billy was.

BILLY FINDS NANNY

Closer and closer she came with her pretty, sweet face showing plainly in the moonlight. Billy scarcely breathed, he was so excited, wondering if she would recognize him, and what she would say when she saw him.

She came straight to the fence and stuck her nose through the rail just above Billy's head before she saw him.

When she did, her eyes dilated with surprise, and then with a bleat of joy, she called:

"Billy! My Billy! Have you come back!" And she commenced to cry as if her heart would break for joy.

No words can express Billy's joy when he felt her tears on his face and her warm nose kissing his cold one, and all Billy could say was, "My darling, you are not married to Satan after all, are you?"

This made Nanny laugh and she called him a silly, old goose.

But what was the matter with Billy? He felt as strong and young as Nanny herself, and had forgotten his thirst and weariness of a few moments ago. Being only a goat, he did not know that happiness is the greatest elixir of life yet discovered.

"Wait a second, Nanny. I can't have this old fence between us," and Billy backed off, gave a spring and was over the fence beside Nanny in no time.

"Oh! Billy, how good it seems to have you back again. Now I have a great surprise for you. Come and see our two 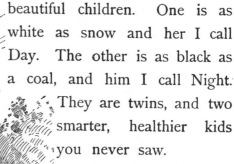 beautiful children. One is as white as snow and her I call Day. The other is as black as a coal, and him I call Night. They are twins, and two smarter, healthier kids you never saw.

"Night is very mischievous and reminds me of you all the time. Ever since you have been gone, I have walked to the fence every night and looked and waited for you to come back and it nearly broke my heart when night after night went by and you did not come."

Billy and Nanny walked over to where their babies were, and Billy assured her that they were the most beautiful kids his eyes had ever rested on, and he felt himself swelling with pride as the father of such handsome kids.

BILLY FINDS NANNY

Nanny led Billy to the stream and while he was quenching his thirst and eating a little of the sweet grass and mint that grew on its bank, they told each other all that had happened since they parted.

I will leave Billy and Nanny here, and my next book will be about Day and Night, Billy and Nanny's kids.

THE END.